Our Two-Week, One-Night Stand

The Loves of Lakeside

Our Two-Week, One-Night Stand

MIMI FRANCIS

4 Horsemen
Publications, Inc.

Dedication

This one is for DeDe. Thank you for being the best mother-in-law in the world. I miss you every day.

Table of Contents

Chapter 1

Cecily

Cecily stared out the window. She hated New York, hated it. She didn't understand why her father insisted she accompany him on his annual trip to the Big Apple. They spent no time together outside of the office, and they didn't talk when they were together anyway. Since her breakup with Lawrence, her father barely spoke to her. His disappointment was palpable and hurtful. She couldn't even bring Sebastian to keep her company. But worse than any of that, her father wouldn't allow her to join him at the board meetings, insisting she wait in his office. Her position in the company—director of company events—didn't require a seat at his board meetings.

Honestly, she was nothing more than a glorified party planner for the company, so coming to New York was a waste of time for Cecily. Behind her, Claude Devereaux, her father, dropped his pen and shoved himself away from his desk. "Have the proposal for the acquisition party on my desk by the time I come back. I want to look it over." His indignant tone mixed with the thickness of his French accent signaled his irritation with her.

Cecily put a smile on her face and turned away from the window. "Of course, Daddy." She took a step toward the door her father was walking toward. "I would love to go with you to the board meeting."

"You're not ready for that kind of responsibility yet, princess," Claude Devereaux said.

"I'm thirty years old, Daddy, with an MBA in business from Stanford. When exactly am I going to be ready?"

"I'm not having this discussion again, Cecily." He straightened his jacket and tie.

"At least let me go to the board meeting with you. You never know, I might have some ideas worth talking about."

"There's no need to attend today's meeting. We're discussing cybersecurity and meeting with the firm that helped us set up the firewalls and safeguards. Nothing to worry yourself about."

"Daddy, if you would give me a chance—"

Claude forcefully interrupted Cecily. "Enough, Cecily. My business is very important to me. I won't entrust it to just anyone."

"But I'm your daughter. No one knows the company or the business like I do. I'm the perfect person to trust. When are you going to realize that?"

Her father rolled his eyes and left without answering her. Cecily paced the room like a caged animal, back and forth in front of the floor-to-ceiling windows, looking out over the skyline she hated.

Six years of college and an MBA, all for nothing because her father would never allow her to run his company. She wasn't the son he'd always wanted so he'd pinned his hopes on a son-in-law, but Cecily crushed those dreams when she dumped Lawrence. Claude pinned all his hopes on Lawrence, the first boyfriend Cecily ever had that her father liked. This was another point of contention between them. No matter how hard she worked or how much she begged, Devereaux Industries was forever out of her reach.

Cecily snatched her purse off the chair and headed for the elevators. She wanted a drink some place where her father wasn't. Outside, she hailed a taxi and asked the driver to take her to the closest bar, where she'd drown her sorrows in vodka martinis.

———

The bar was a little more than half full when Cecily walked in. She pushed through the crowd, nodding and smiling, as she made her way to a seat at the bar and ordered a drink. She smiled gratefully at the bartender when he set her vodka martini in front of her. A sigh of relief escaped her when the cool liquor slid down her throat.

Cecily watched the five o'clock, after work crowd fill the dance floor, as her foot tapped with the thumping beat of the music. When a cute guy asked her to dance, she readily agreed. It had been too long since she'd had any fun. If Cecily had to be in this godforsaken city, she could at least enjoy herself.

Hours passed; the sun set, and the dark bar grew darker. She lost track of how many songs she danced to and how many drinks she had. Free of her father's disapproving glares and archaic ideas—if only for a little while—Cecily let herself go.

Suddenly, a man drew her eye as soon as he walked through the door. He was tall, maybe 6'3", blond, muscular, mid-thirties, and drop-dead gorgeous in a Captain America-kind of way. Tight jeans clung to his thick thighs and a black leather jacket covered his bulging arms and broad shoulders. Both the men and the women stared at him, stopping in their tracks with their mouths hanging open to stare at the blond god making his way across the room. The crowd split to let him pass, and he walked right through them like he owned the place. He yanked his jacket off and sat at the corner of the bar.

Cecily kept an eye on him as she danced until the crowd grew and merged in front of her, obscuring her view. She danced for a few more minutes before making her way to the edge of the dance floor. He stared at her, and heat flooded her cheeks. Eyes downcast, she eased into her seat on the opposite side of the bar. When Cecily looked up, she looked right into a pair of gorgeous dark blue eyes. Nerves overtook her, and she looked away. She caught the bartender's attention and ordered another drink.

"Put her drink on my tab." His voice was deep, one of those voices you never tired of hearing. He stood beside her chair, close enough that she could smell the spicy scent of his aftershave and see the rippling muscles under his shirt. Cecily couldn't stop staring at him.

He was the most gorgeous man she had ever seen. Even though he stood well over six feet, he moved with cat-like grace and ease. He had broad shoulders that tapered down to a tiny, tight waist, where she could see his well-toned abs through his too-small shirt. He pushed a hand through his short blond hair as his cobalt blue eyes danced over her.

"Mind if I sit down?" he asked, gesturing to the empty seat beside her. One side of his mouth pulled up in a sexy, little smirk and in that moment, Cecily knew exactly how her evening would end.

She hadn't expected to meet someone, not in New York, but she wouldn't look a gift horse in the mouth. It would only be for one night, like the other men she'd slept with during the last few months. She would talk to this guy and have some fun, maybe a lot of fun if the evening went as she hoped.

"Not at all." She held out her hand. "My name is Cecily."

"Nice to meet you, Cecily." The smirk grew into a grin. "I'm Lincoln." His large hand encompassed hers. He held it longer than necessary, squeezing it before releasing it.

Lincoln sat on the stool beside her, and they chatted for a few minutes about nothing important while they sipped their drinks: the weather, the crowd in the bar, and the score of the Mets game playing on the bar TV.

The music swelled, and an upbeat song she loved pumped through the speakers in the corner. Cecily swayed side to side, her foot tapping. "What do you say we dance?"

Lincoln laughed and shook his head. "I don't know; I'm not much of a dancer."

Cecily stood up and grabbed his hand. "You've never danced with me. It'll be fun, I promise."

He shrugged, set his beer on the bar, and let her lead him by the hand to the dance floor. She took his hands, placed them on her hips, and eased closer to him. She took a deep breath and shimmied to the music, sidling closer to Lincoln and letting the music control her movements.

Lincoln stood in front of her, stiff and unmoving. He squeezed her hips so hard, it hurt.

"Relax, Lincoln."

"I'm not so good at this," he muttered. "Are you sure about this? Maybe we should go back and sit down."

Cecily laughed, pushed up on her toes, and pressed her lips to Lincoln's ear. "Shut up and dance with me."

Lincoln gulped and pulled her tight against his body, his focus on her and her alone. He squeezed her hips again as she wiggled against him. He bit his lip, and a faint blush colored his cheeks.

Despite his reluctance, Cecily kept Lincoln on the dance floor for several songs, the two of them moving fluidly with the music. Lincoln was a fabulous dancer. Even though he hadn't wanted to dance with her, he appeared to be enjoying himself.

Emboldened by the way Lincoln looked at her, and how the heat of his stare caused a tingling ache between her legs, she put her hands on his cheeks and kissed him. It was gentle at first, her way of testing the waters and gauging his interest. The kiss only lasted a few seconds before it exploded, and they began exploring each other with reckless abandon.

It was as if they were alone in the crowded room: hands all over each other, her tongue in his mouth, the taste of beer and mint gum filling her mouth. Unable to stay quiet, Cecily moaned quietly.

Lincoln pushed away from her, glanced around, and then he pulled her down a dimly lit, secluded hallway leading to the bathrooms. No one was coming or going, so they were alone.

With one more glance over his shoulder, he pushed her against the wall between the bathroom door, grabbed the bottom of her skirt, and hiked it up. He put his hand on her ass and squeezed, groaning when he grazed her bare skin. His mouth covered hers with a kiss like nothing she'd ever experienced. He kneaded her breast through the silky fabric of her blouse, drawing a groan from her as her nipples hardened. She squirmed against him and her back arched as she pushed herself against Lincoln's warm body.

"Let's get out of here," he whispered in her ear. He kissed her neck, his lips sliding down to her collarbone where he nibbled at the space where her neck and shoulder met.

Her brain—along with her mouth—shut down as Lincoln's lips moved over her skin. She threw her head back so he could have better access to her neck. The stubble on his cheeks and chin rubbed deliciously against her, burning in the best way possible and obliterating all coherent thought. There was only Lincoln.

Cecily felt the hard line of his erection as Lincoln pressed his hips into hers. He tangled his fingers in her hair and nipped at her bottom lip.

"Cecily. Look at me."

She looked at him with hooded eyes, her heart pounding, and the whoosh of blood rushing in her ears.

Lincoln licked his lips. "If we don't get out of here soon, I'm gonna take you right here against this wall, and I won't give a shit who sees it."

That was what she'd been hoping to hear. She smiled, slid her hand between their bodies, and rested it on Lincoln's hard shaft trapped between them. Raising up slightly on her toes, she wrapped her hand around the back of his neck, pulled him down, and kissed him.

"Do you think you're man enough to handle me? I might be more of a woman than you're used to." She squeezed him gently, his cock twitching behind the zipper of his jeans.

Lincoln growled low in the back of his throat and moved in to kiss her, but at the last second, she turned her head with a teasing smile on her lips. He moaned, grabbed her wrists, and held them over her head, his grip like an iron vise. He pushed his hips into hers, grinding against her and drawing a moan from Cecily, as unexpected heat shot through to her core and settled in the pit of her stomach. She ached with need.

"I don't think it'll be a problem, sweetheart. I will leave you spent and more satisfied than you can even imagine. You'll scream my name when you cum." His hips moved in a slow circle, his enormous cock straining to be released. "The question is, do you want me to do that right here, against this wall, or do you want me to take you back to your place so I can give you the ride of your life?"

"My hotel is around the corner," she whispered breathlessly.

Lincoln kissed her throat, right beneath her jaw. "Good choice." He took a step back, straightened her blouse and skirt, then he took her hand and strolled back to the bar.

"Before we go, I have to tell you something," Cecily said.

"Okay."

"This is a one-time thing. Just tonight. I'm not interested in anything more or anything permanent. I'm just looking for some fun."

"Perfect, because that is all I'm looking for, sweetheart. I'm not interested in any kind of relationship, either. One night only." Lincoln said. "And trust me, I promise it will be fun."

Cecily downed her drink and picked up her purse. "I'm down the street at the Conrad."

He pressed a kiss to her cheek. "Let's go."

Chapter 2

Cecily

Cecily didn't remember the walk back to the hotel. All she could think about was her hand in Lincoln's, the way her lips still burned from his kisses, and how her body was on fire everywhere he had touched. He kept his distance as they walked through the lobby and took the elevator upstairs, only holding her hand. After they got off at her floor, he put his hand on her waist and waited patiently behind her as she unlocked the hotel room door. Once they were inside, Lincoln held her hand while he slipped the "Do Not Disturb" sign over the handle and pushed the door closed. He spun around and pounced on her, a gleam in his eye.

"Bedroom?"

Cecily pointed over her shoulder. Lincoln took her hand and led her through the hotel suite to the adjoining bedroom. She stopped at the end of the bed while Lincoln walked to the other side of the room, turned on the bedside table lamp, and turned back to her.

He removed his shirt, tossing it on the floor as he toed off his shoes, unbuckled his belt, and unzipped his jeans. Cecily caught a brief glimpse of dark blond hair dropping into the top of the v behind the zipper. Her heart skipped a beat when she realized he wasn't wearing any underwear. He kept his eyes on her as she crossed the room to stand in front of him.

"Why are you still dressed?" he asked gruffly.

She shrugged her shoulders and shook her head. Her stomach flipped, and her hands shook, something she didn't expect. One-night stands didn't make her nervous; they never had. But Lincoln was different. She did not know why, but he was.

"Cecily?"

"Sorry," she mumbled. She reached for the lamp Lincoln had turned on, but he caught her hand and stopped her.

"What are you doing?" he demanded.

"I'm turning off the light."

Even though Cecily had grown to love and accept herself the way she was, she didn't have sex with the lights on. That confidence and acceptance slipped when she was in the bedroom. Years of teasing and self-doubt were hard to shake, especially with feeling sexy. Her last boyfriend, Lawrence, hadn't helped; he never made her feel sexy. They never made love with the lights on because he said he didn't need to see her when they had sex.

"I love you *despite* your flaws," Lawrence would tell her. Those flaws Lawrence referred to were nothing more than her curvy, larger-than-average body.

The damage Lawrence did was the reason she hadn't dated anyone seriously since their breakup six months earlier. She didn't trust anyone. Most men only cared about sex, something that could be done with the lights off and forgotten about the next day. She was forgettable, so it was easier to sleep with them and walk away; that way, she stayed whole.

"Leave it on," Lincoln said. "I want to see you."

Cecily opened her mouth to argue, but he cut her off with a kiss, his hands sliding over her body. He cupped her ass and dragged her close, emphasizing his desire for her by rubbing his body against hers.

"Now take off your clothes."

The tone of his voice left no room for argument. She hurried to remove her skirt and blouse, dropping them on the floor beside his. She resisted the urge to cover herself with her hands. Before she took off anything else, his mouth was on hers, his tongue buried in her mouth. Lincoln sat on the edge of the bed in front of her, removed her bra and tossed it aside. He thumbed her nipple as he kneaded her breast, then his tongue darted out and caressed the erect nipple. Lincoln hooked his finger in her lacy, black underwear and pushed them down her legs as he kissed his way down her body.

Cecily jumped and tried to push him away when his tongue flicked against her warm center at the apex of her thighs. Lincoln wrapped his arm around her thighs, holding her in place. He looked up at her, confused.

"What's wrong?" he asked. His voice was deeper, gruffer, sexier.

"I ... I ... just let me turn off the light," she answered. Cecily reached for it again, but in one swift move, Lincoln tossed her onto the bed and trapped her beneath him.

"I said I want to see you," he reiterated, his blue eyes boring into hers.

"But why?"

"You're gorgeous, Cecily," he whispered. His breath was hot against her ear, bringing goosebumps to the surface of her skin. Lincoln slipped his hand between her legs and caressed her as he talked, making it difficult to concentrate on his words. "I want to watch you come undone, watch your beautiful face as you cum, and watch this gorgeous body move as I ... do ... this."

His long middle finger slid slowly inside her, the palm of his hand pressed against her, as he moved in tight, small circles.

She moaned while her hips grinded against his hand, her eyes rolling back in her head as he massaged her. Lincoln smiled, his dark blue eyes sparkling as he watched her.

His mouth closed over her breast and his tongue swirled around the nipple, sucking it greedily. Cecily clutched the blankets in her hands as the tension built, and wound her body tighter and tighter, bringing her closer to the edge with every movement. Lincoln moved down her body, kissing her everywhere, as his finger continued to pump, sending tingles storming through her entire body. No one had ever done this to her; no one had ever brought her to the peak of climax so easily. He hovered over her wet core, his warm breath blowing over her. He glanced up at her, with that damn, sexy smirk on his face.

"Hold on to something, sweetheart," he said. His tongue flicked out, dancing over her sensitive nub and driving her wild with need. He thrust another finger into her, and her hips leaped off the bed. He pushed her back down, positioned his head between her legs, and worked her open with his mouth.

Cecily held the back of his head, grinding against his face. Her startled gasps interspersed with cries of his name, filling the room as she hurtled toward her climax. When he put his palm flat on her stomach and moved forward, pushing his tongue deeper into her, she lost it. Something between a scream and a squeal burst out of her, as an orgasm to beat all orgasms blew through her.

When Lincoln pulled away, Cecily trembled, her heart pounding out of control and she couldn't catch her breath. He licked his lips as he crawled back up the bed and laid beside her. Cecily took a few moments to catch her breath and collect herself before she rolled to her side, eased her hand past the waistband of Lincoln's jeans, and took hold of him. She stroked his cock, silently marveling at his size as his hips moved, thrusting into her hand.

"Mm, that's it, gorgeous. That's perfect." He rested his forehead against hers and squeezed his eyes closed, with his mouth open and lips glistening.

She loved the sound of his voice, deep and sexy, praising her as she touched him. She pushed his pants down over his hips, giggling as he impatiently kicked them off. He took a condom from his pocket, sat up, and moved to the top of the bed, his back against the headboard.

"Come here," he said, as he slid the condom down his length.

Cecily shook her head. "No. It's okay, really—"

Lincoln grabbed her arm, pulled her close, and cut her off with another kiss. "I want this, Cecily. I want you like this, right now. So, stop talking and get over here. I want to hold on to that pretty ass while you ride me."

Cecily crawled into his lap and straddled him, moaning as she slid down his hard cock. He filled her completely. She slid forward and moved carefully, not sure how much Lincoln could take.

He moaned, one hand gripping her ass so hard she was sure it would leave marks. His fingers tangled in her hair, tugging her head back to stare into her eyes. He yanked her forward, thrusting into her, hard.

"No need to be gentle. I can take whatever you want to give me," he said.

Cecily nodded, pressed her knees into the bed on either side of his hips, and ground down onto him. His hips jerked, pumping into her. She planted her hands on his shoulders, dug her nails into his shoulders, and rode him hard. She didn't let up, her breasts bouncing up and down as they brushed against his naked chest. As her clit pressed against his pelvic bone, the sensation pushed her toward another orgasm. Lincoln pulled her hips down and thrust so deep into her, she thought she might pass out.

Lincoln groaned. "Fuck yeah, that's it. Just like that. That's what I want." He panted and sweat ran down his neck and chest, the muscles in his thighs hard and tight as his cock slid in and out of her. "Come on, let me feel you cum all over me." He slipped a hand between their bodies, pushed his back against the headboard, and braced himself with his feet while he pounded into her. His cock brushed her sweet spot while he thumbed her clit until she let go with an obscene moan, coming harder than she ever had before. Her nails dug into his shoulders as she held on, wave after wave of unbelievable pleasure washing over her.

Lincoln grunted and thrusted up into her one more time, groaning as his own orgasm swept over him. His head fell to Cecily's shoulder, and his entire body shuddered as he came.

"Wow," she mumbled once she could breathe again. She kissed his neck several times before she sat up. She tried to move off him and cover herself, but Lincoln held her against him as he rolled to his side. He kissed her, his hands running over her curves while his eyes followed his hands.

"I'm not done with you," he whispered.

"Oh, yeah?"

Lincoln smirked. "Yeah. I hope you didn't have any plans tonight."

"Nothing I can't cancel."

"Great, let's spend the rest of the night right here."

"That sounds amazing," she whispered as she laid her head on his shoulder.

———

The incessant buzzing of her cellphone dragged her from sleep. She opened one eye, but it wasn't on the bedside table where she usually kept it. Maybe it was in her purse. Not that she had any intention of getting out of bed and answering it. Thankfully, after a few seconds, it stopped.

Cecily rolled onto her back and stretched. Her muscles ached, but in the best way possible. She looked to her right but saw she was alone in the bed.

"Lincoln?" She sat up, the covers pooling in her lap. "Lincoln, are you here?"

No answer. He was gone.

She wasn't surprised. Cecily made it quite clear this was a one-night situation and nothing more, and he'd agreed. She didn't mind; she was flying back to Montana today, so New York could kiss her ass.

A loud pounding on the door startled her and dragged her from the bed. It had to be her father, come to collect her for her flight back to Montana. She was halfway across the room when she heard her Claude. "Cecily Camille Devereaux! Open this door right now, young lady."

She rolled her eyes. It was going to be a long ride to the airport.

Chapter 3

Cecily

"Cecily!" Nate shouted. "Where's Sebastian?"

She slipped onto the barstool and gave Nate, the bar's owner and bartender, a smile. "He's home," she answered. "He was being an asshole. I wasn't in the mood to deal with him, so I told him to stay home and think about his attitude."

Nate laughed and set a vodka martini in front of her. "Think it'll work?"

"Probably not. He's stubborn as hell. He doesn't enjoy staying home, though, so he might behave for a few days. I'll see what kind of mood he's in when I get back."

"Are you hungry?" Nate asked. "I could make you something to eat."

"I'm fine. Thanks."

Nate narrowed his eyes. "When's the last time you ate?"

Cecily rolled her eyes. "I don't know. Two, maybe three hours ago. What difference does it make?"

"I'm just looking out for you, that's all." Nate wiped down the bar in front of her, even though it wasn't dirty. He kept his bar spotless.

"I'm a big girl. I can take care of myself." She grabbed her drink and took a swallow, doing anything to not look Nate in the eyes.

Her friend frowned. "How long have we been friends?"

"Too long?"

"I'm serious, Cecily."

She smiled at Nate. "Since your dad bought the bar and you moved to town. So, a little over two years? Why?"

"I know you, and you don't look fine," Nate said. "You look tired."

"I'm fine," she repeated. "I promise." She knew Nate didn't believe her, but she didn't have the energy to argue.

Nate didn't need to know the stress was killing her. For the last three months, Lawrence had called her nonstop, all day every day, begging for another chance. Her father threatened to cut her off if she didn't patch things up with Lawrence and get a proper job—which, to him, meant taking back her old job as Devereaux Industries' glorified party planner. Living alone in the mansion on the lake was depressing and, more than anything else, it reminded her that her mother had passed away. She missed her mom.

A loud cheer erupted from the corner, making Cecily jump and her drink slosh over the side of her glass. "Damn it."

Nate laughed. "Are they too loud for you, princess?"

Cecily snorted and threw a straw at Nate. He knew she hated that—her father sometimes called her princess, and it drove her crazy. Nate liked to tease.

"What's going on over there?"

"Van's bachelor party."

"Van's bachelor party? I should have known. I just came from Serena's bridal shower; it was tamer than those guys watching the Mariners and Yankees, though. I can't believe the wedding is Monday."

"Seems like yesterday that Serena started working at Lakeside College, doesn't it?" Nate said. "I can't believe she's lived here for almost a year."

"Has it been a year already?" Cecily asked. "I met her and Van six months ago when I moved back to town and interviewed for a teaching position at the college. We hit it off, immediately. She's so sweet and perfect for Van. I can't wait for the wedding."

"It came up fast, didn't it? Are you going?"

"Yeah, you?"

Nate nodded. "I agreed to tend bar for Van, my wedding gift to the couple. And my roommate, Mason is taking the wedding photos. Hey, how's the job hunt going? Any luck?"

Cecily took another drink. "No. My father is to blame for that. I think he's sabotaging my efforts to find work with another company. I've done a few things for Lakeside College, but with it being summer, the university president, Charlie, doesn't have much for me to do."

"So, your father is keeping you from getting a job with another company, and he won't let you work for his?" Nate shook his head. "I'll never understand Claude Devereaux."

She sighed. "It's a power trip thing. He wants me under his thumb, but he doesn't want to give me anything meaningful to do. Making me a party planner is supposed to appease me, but he hates the fact that I want more. In his eyes, I *am* working for him, but it's not anything important."

"I'm sorry." Nate patted her arm.

Cecily shrugged, uncomfortable with someone feeling sorry for her. She cleared her throat and pointed to the bottles of alcohol behind Nate.

"Can you get me another drink? Actually, on second thought, how about some fries?"

"You got it." Nate poured her another drink before heading toward the kitchen, stopping every few feet to check in with the other customers in the restaurant.

She picked up her drink and took another sip. Exhausted, she closed her eyes and took a deep breath. The last time she'd had a good night's sleep was in New York. Thinking about New York inevitably led to thinking about Lincoln, and that was never good.

Lincoln was always on her mind since their time together, and it scared her. Never once had a one-night stand gotten under her skin like this one had. She couldn't stop thinking about him and the things they'd done. She wished it could happen again. Spending the night in bed with Lincoln had been amazing. If only she'd gotten his last name, his number, something. She longed to hear his deep, sexy voice whispering in her ear.

Someone backed into her and jostled her elbow, knocking her out of her seat and spilling her drink onto the bar and into her lap. Cecily stumbled to her feet, praying she wouldn't land on her ass. She cursed under her breath and grabbed a stack of napkins.

"Oh, my God. I'm so sorry."

Cecily froze, choking on the words she'd been about to say. It wasn't possible, not when he was over two-thousand miles away on the other side of the country. It couldn't be him, unless thinking about him had magically summoned him. If that was the case, he would have shown up three months ago. She turned as everything was moving in slow motion.

Standing in front of her was the tall, blond, muscular, drop-dead gorgeous in a Captain America-kind of way man she had first seen three months ago.

"Lincoln?"

"Holy shit! Cecily?"

"What are you—?"

"How the hell—?"

Lincoln seemed just as surprised to see her as she was to see him. One hand brushed against her arm as he moved closer to her, a smile spreading across his chiseled face.

Cecily stepped into his personal space and kissed his cheek, anxious to get close to him. It wasn't easy to keep her hands to herself. She wanted to touch him, caress him, and remind herself why this man was constantly on her mind. Lincoln gestured for her to speak.

"What are you doing here?" she asked.

"My best friend is getting married in two days." He took her hand and rubbed his thumb across her knuckles. The simple gesture sent a tingle of desire down her spine and reminded her of their time together.

"Van?"

The surprised look on Lincoln's face made her giggle. "I'm not a mind reader or something," she said. "I know

Serena, and the bar owner, Nate, is a friend of mine. He told me about the bachelor party."

"Of course," Lincoln said. He guided her to her seat and sat down beside her. "I can't believe you're in a tiny town in Montana. I never expected to run into you here, or anywhere. What a small world."

"I could say the same thing about you. Lakeside, Montana, is pretty far from New York City."

Lincoln chuckled. "Van loves this place; it's his home, and I would not miss my best friend's wedding because it's in the middle of nowhere."

Cecily laughed. "It is off the beaten path. I'm glad we ran into each other, though."

"Okay, so you know why I'm here," Lincoln said. "What are you doing in Montana?"

"I live here," she explained. "My family owns a home nearby."

"I never would have guessed. You don't seem like a Montana kind of girl."

"I'm not really a Montana girl; it's more like an adopted home. We have a vacation home on the lake. I sort of borrowed it six months ago and haven't left. My family is from France. My father moved to the United States before I was born. We've lived all over the world."

"Military?"

Cecily shrugged. "Something like that."

She wouldn't answer that question. She didn't tell people—especially men she slept with—who her father was. It complicated things when they found out she was the heir to a billion-dollar empire. The way things had gotten complicated with Lawrence and the reason he wouldn't leave her alone.

Lincoln didn't press the issue but leaned on the bar and propped his head up on his hand. "It's good to see you, Cecily. Fantastic."

Cecily brushed a hand through Lincoln's messy hair and stroked his face. "I'm glad to see you too. More than you know."

"I've been thinking about you a lot since that night in New York," he said.

"Really?" she asked.

"Really." Lincoln ran his hand up her leg. "You're pretty unforgettable, sweetheart," he whispered.

Heat rushed through her from head to toe. Lincoln's presence was a dream come true, the man she'd thought about nonstop for the last three months sitting right in front of her. "I could say the same about you," Cecily replied coyly.

Lincoln cleared his throat and his cheeks flushed pink. "I am sorry about your drink. Let me buy you another one. Vodka martini, right?"

He remembered what she drank. *God, could he be any more perfect?* She swallowed and nodded.

"Yep. Vodka martini."

Chapter 4

Lincoln

His trip from New York was a nightmare. The connecting flight to Chicago landed late, causing him to miss his flight into Kalispell, Montana. He spent an uncomfortable night in the airport, waiting to catch a standby flight into Missoula, Montana. It wasn't his first choice and it was a longer drive, but there was nothing else he could do. It was eight hours before a seat on another flight was available. Once Lincoln landed in Missoula, the rental company didn't have an SUV available so he settled for a compact car that was far too small for his 6'3" frame. By the time he pulled into Van's driveway at nine the next morning, his legs, shoulders, and back ached so much. He wanted sleep, a shower, and a beer, not necessarily in that order.

When he approached the door, Lincoln knocked once, even though he was sure no one was home. He and Van had talked several times during his layover in Chicago, so his friend knew he would be late. Van told Lincoln to make himself at home while he and Serena were at work. Fortunately, Lincoln had his own key to Van's place, so he let himself into the small condo.

It was quiet: no Serena and no Van. Soldier, Van's Belgian Malinois, wasn't there either; no doubt he was at Van's side. Lincoln breathed a sigh of relief and trudged upstairs, dumping his things in the spare bedroom and ducking into the bathroom. If he wanted to enjoy himself at Van's bachelor party tonight, he needed to sleep.

Lincoln still had a hard time believing Van was getting married. After Van's first wife, Adelaide was murdered, Lincoln wondered if Van would ever leave his house again, let alone meet someone, fall in love, and get married. Then Serena came into his life and changed everything for the better. He couldn't have been happier for his best friend.

He showered and shaved, downed a bottle of water from the fridge, and fell into bed. After closing his eyes, he passed out in a deep sleep.

—

A wet, sloppy tongue sliding up his cheek drew Lincoln from sleep. He groaned and opened one eye. Soldier stood over him, his tongue hanging out of his mouth.

"Hey, boy," Lincoln mumbled. "Where's your owner?"

Soldier bounded out the door, stood in the hall, and barked once. Lincoln dragged himself out of bed and followed the dog downstairs.

"He lives!" Serena jumped off the couch and hugged him tight. "It's so good to see you."

"What time is it?" he asked.

"Almost four," Van answered. He grabbed Lincoln's hand, shook it, and pulled him into a hug. "It's good to see you, brother."

"You too."

It wasn't just good to see Van; it was great. They'd been friends since childhood, grew up together, joined the army together, and started a security consulting business when they returned to New York. Lincoln tried to keep their friendship together when Van moved to Montana after Adelaide's death, but it was a struggle. Van pushed everyone away, except his dog, after his wife's death. Thank God Serena came along and pulled Van out of his self-imposed imprisonment.

"You ready for tonight?" Lincoln asked.

Van rolled his eyes. "I guess. You know how I love to be the center of attention."

"It's a bunch of guys getting together for drinks at the bar," Serena interjected. "It's not like Nate is having a parade down Main Street for you."

Lincoln laughed, as he loved how Serena called Van on his shit. He clapped his friend on the back. "It'll be fun. A bunch of guys shooting the shit. No pressure, no demanding women around—."

Serena punched Lincoln playfully on the arm. "Watch it, mister." She wrapped her arms around Van's waist and kissed him on the cheek. "It's only for a couple of hours. You don't want to be here with a bunch of giggling women oohing and ahhing over lingerie, do you?"

"I do," Lincoln cheerfully interjected.

"We need to find you a girlfriend," Van muttered.

Lincoln shook his head. "Nope; that is not happening. I am not interested in a relationship. Too complicated."

Serena opened her mouth—probably to ask why—but Lincoln turned and sprinted up the stairs. He wasn't interested in opening those old wounds. "I'll go change so we can go," he called over his shoulder.

———

According to Van, Time Out was the most popular bar and grill in Lakeside. He didn't bother to mention it was the only bar and grill in Lakeside, but no sense in bringing up the obvious.

Time Out was owned by Nathan "Nate" Owens, a twenty-three-year-old entrepreneur from Great Falls, Montana. His father helped him buy the bar when he was twenty-one and he'd turned it into a thriving business in less than two years. Van said he was a "nice kid," and he wasn't wrong.

Nate sectioned off the back corner of the bar and laid out quite the spread—stuff like burgers, nachos, fries, and chicken wings. If it was bad for you, it was there. The drinks flowed nonstop: beer, wine, water, soda, you name it, it was available. Nate assured them if they needed anything, he would get it.

Lincoln was thrilled Van agreed to have a bachelor party. Van had always kept to himself, especially after the death of his first wife. He'd been a hermit when he met Serena, and obviously things had changed since he took the security job at Lakeside College. While it wasn't an enormous party, there were still nine people in attendance, including Nate. It eased Lincoln's mind that Van had friends he could turn to other than him, even if they were people from work.

"Are you having fun?" Van asked after two hours of pool, baseball, food, and drink.

"Yes, of course." Lincoln slapped Van on the shoulder. "What about you?"

"Don't tell Serena, but yes, I am."

Lincoln chuckled. "I'm totally telling Serena you said that. No secrets between married couples."

"Speaking of no secrets, my lovely fiancée wants to know why you don't have a girlfriend."

Lincoln rolled his eyes. "Did you tell her I don't *want* a girlfriend?"

"Yes, but Serena is ... persistent."

"She's not going to set me up, is she?"

Van shrugged. "I can't make any promises."

Lincoln chugged his beer. "I need another drink." He needed something stronger than a beer, so he spun around and headed for the bar.

"Bring me a scotch and soda!" Van called after him.

Lincoln turned around and waved at Van. A second later, not realizing how close he was to the bar, he bumped into someone behind him. A startled squeak erupted in his ear, followed by a lot of cursing. A young woman stood beside him, her back turned, as she muttered curses under her breath and wiped her clothes with a stack of napkins.

"Oh, my God. I'm so sorry," Lincoln apologized.

The woman swung around, a startled look on her face and her gorgeous mouth hanging open.

"Lincoln?"

"Holy shit! Cecily?" He couldn't believe his last New York one-night stand was in a little town in Montana and that he had run into her.

"What are you—?"

"How the hell—?"

Montana was the last place in the world he expected to run into this woman, as he thought he'd never see her again. But Cecily had lingered in his mind since they'd met. It was the first time he regretted not getting a woman's number so he could call her again.

Now she stood in front of him, her long black hair plaited in a braid down her back, her gray eyes sparkling, and her mouth open in surprise. He wanted to kiss her. Hell, he wanted to do more than that.

Cecily stepped close—so close the sweet smell of her pomegranate and vanilla perfume enveloped him—and kissed his cheek. God, she was too close. He clenched his hands and reminded himself they were in a public place.

"What are you doing here?" she asked.

Lincoln grabbed her hand, desperate to touch her, and rubbed his thumb over her knuckles. He forced himself to concentrate and answer her question. "My best friend is getting married in two days."

The dimple in her cheek became more prominent when she smiled. "Van?"

Is she a mind reader?

He must have looked surprised because Cecily giggled. "I'm not a mind reader or something. I know Serena, and the bar owner, Nate, is a friend of mine. He told me about the bachelor party."

"Of course." *How was it she could echo his thoughts?* He kept hold of her hand and guided her back to the bar. He sat on the stool beside her. "I can't believe you're in a tiny town in Montana. I certainly never expected to run into you here, or anywhere. What a small world."

Nice going, Linc. Remind her a few more times that she was just a one-night stand.

Her cheeks turned a faint shade of pink. "I could say the same thing about you. Lakeside, Montana is pretty far from New York City."

He laughed. "Van loves this place; it's his home, and I would not miss my best friend's wedding because it's in the middle of nowhere. I thought it would be a good time for a vacation, too."

She couldn't argue with him. "It is off the beaten path. I'm glad we ran into each other, though."

"Okay, so you know why I'm here," Lincoln said. "What are you doing in Montana?"

"I live here. My family owns a home nearby."

Lincoln shook his head. "I never would have guessed. You don't seem like a Montana kind of girl."

Cecily volunteered some more information, though she dodged his more probing questions about her family and her childhood. He decided not to push the issue. Let her have her secrets; she must have a reason.

Lincoln leaned on the bar, thinking, *Maybe this trip to Lakeside wouldn't be a complete bust.* "It's good to see you, Cecily. Fantastic."

Cecily pushed a hand through his hair and stroked a finger down his face. "I'm glad to see you too. More than you know."

"I've been thinking about you a lot since that night in New York."

"Really?" The smile on her face made his heart leap.

Lincoln nodded. "Really." He stroked her leg, leaned close, and dropped his voice to a whisper. "You're pretty unforgettable, sweetheart."

A flirty smile danced across her lips. "I could say the same about you."

He cleared his throat. "I am sorry about your drink. Let me buy you another one. Vodka martini, right?"

Chapter 5

Lincoln

"*I*'m going to the ladies' room," Cecily said, after he ordered her drink. She kissed Lincoln's cheek, grabbed her purse, and disappeared down the hall.

Warmth spread through his chest, and his heart pounded. No woman had ever done that to him. Since his ex-wife Cat broke his heart, ten years ago he'd become the perpetual bachelor, destined to be alone forever. He was okay with that; serious relationships weren't his cup of tea, not anymore. However, these feelings for Cecily were different and unexpected. *Cecily* was different and unexpected.

What the hell is this?

Van eased into the seat Cecily just vacated across from Lincoln, and Soldier laid down next to his feet. He smiled at his best friend. "You disappeared," he said. "I thought you left."

"Shit. Sorry, I was talking to—."

"I saw her." Van cleared his throat and shifted nervously. "Pretty girl."

"Yes, she is."

"Do me a favor and don't sleep with her, and then blow her off right away, okay? She's going to the wedding."

"Wait, you know her?" Lincoln said in shock.

"She's a friend of Serena's. I think she works at Lakeside College. So, yes, I know her."

"Holy shit." Lincoln scrubbed a hand over his face and shook his head.

Van's eyes narrowed. "What did you do?"

Lincoln glanced around before he leaned forward and dropped his voice to a whisper. "I already slept with her."

Van pinched the bridge of his nose. "You slept with her? How the hell did you manage that? You've been in town less than twenty-four hours."

"I didn't sleep with her *here*. I slept with her in New York. Three months ago. I met her in a bar, and we went back to her hotel."

"You slept with her three months ago? And now you run into her in a bar in Lakeside, Montana? Jesus, talk about a small world."

Lincoln shook his head. "It was the day of my last meeting with Devereaux. The bar was close to his New York office. The meeting stressed me out, so I went there to unwind—."

"Met Cecily and slept with her. How do you do it, Lincoln? Only you could find the one woman in New York City who lives in Montana." Van snapped his fingers. "You didn't think you'd see her again, did you?"

"Would you stop doing that?" Lincoln sharply replied. It drove him nuts that Van always knew what he was thinking, sometimes before he knew it.

Van chuckled. "Sorry. But I know you better than you know yourself."

"Which pisses me off. You're right. I didn't think I'd see her again, okay? I'm glad I did, though. We had a great time. A really great time. I wouldn't mind spending time with her while I'm in Lakeside."

Van raised an eyebrow, then changed the subject. "I came over here to tell you I'm gonna head home. I've had enough of being the center of attention for one night." He put a set of keys on the bar in front of Lincoln. "These are the extra keys to Serena's condo, since she kicked us out of my place until after the wedding."

He slipped the keys into his pocket. "Thanks."

"Just do me a favor, okay?" Van said.

"Okay. What?"

"Don't do anything stupid." He whistled, and Soldier moved to his side. The dog pushed his head against Van's hand. "I might have to spend time this woman after you go home."

Lincoln chuckled. "I won't, I promise."

———

This qualifies as stupid.

Lincoln had Cecily pushed up against her car in the bar's parking lot, one hand on her ass and the other under the edge of her sweater, gripping her waist. She groaned into his mouth as he kissed her. He broke off the kiss, but he didn't release her.

"I should go," he whispered.

"I don't want you to go," Cecily said. "Stay here." She wrapped her arms around his waist. "Better yet, come back to my place."

That would definitely be stupid.

"I can't," he said. "I should go."

She pouted, her bottom lip pushing out looking plump and pink. "Am I going to see you again?"

He took her chin in his hand and kissed her. "Hell, yes."

Stupid.

Lincoln pulled his phone out of his pocket. "What's your number?"

Cecily rattled it off. She checked his screen to make sure he had it correct. "You'll call me, won't you?"

"Definitely. And if you don't hear from me, you call me." He typed his name in a message and sent it to Cecily's number, then he kissed her one last time, opened her car door, and helped her inside. He didn't climb into his rental car until she rounded the corner and was out of sight.

Lincoln wasn't tired when he returned to the condo. Soldier met him at the door, his hackles raised and growling until he realized it was Lincoln. The dog huffed, turned around, and headed down the hall. Lincoln followed Soldier down the hall to the master bedroom where Van was sound asleep. Soldier dropped to the floor beside the bed and closed his eyes.

Serena relegated the two of them to her old condo across the street from Van's until after the wedding. Lincoln wasn't familiar with her place, so he took a few minutes to look around until he found his stuff in the room across from Van's. He wasn't tired after sleeping all day, so he grabbed a beer from the kitchen and went out onto the patio. The view was almost as good as Van's, so he took a seat and stared at the water of Flathead Lake lapping against the shore.

Lincoln checked his watch. It was after eleven on a Friday night and he was exhausted. He was in Lakeside for two weeks, his first real vacation in years. Coincidentally, that was how long it usually took him to decide he didn't want to date one of the multitude of women he'd slept with over the years. Cecily would be no different: they could hang out, have fun, and, of course, have sex. When it was over, he could go back to New York and back to living his life without Cecily taking up any more space in his head. It would be a good way to cleanse his system of her.

He leaned his head back on the chair and stared at the stars. They always seemed so much brighter in Montana, especially without the skyscrapers, smog, and bright lights of New York dimming their intensity.

Maybe I should move up here.

It wasn't the first time he'd thought about giving up the insanity of the Big Apple for small-town life in Montana. Now that they'd taken care of the business by selling it to the security company in Hollywood, he could seriously consider getting out of New York. Of course, that was before he knew Cecily was here. If he moved to Montana, she might get the idea he was interested in some kind of relationship.

Would that be such a bad thing? Maybe it's time to —

He cut off the voice in his head by downing the rest of his beer. He scrubbed a hand over his face and rose to his feet.

Two weeks; that's it. Just two weeks. Like a two-week one-night stand.

He dropped the empty bottle in the recycle can and headed for bed, falling asleep before his head hit the pillow.

Chapter 6

Cecily

Cecily heard Sebastian before she saw him. He didn't like to be left home alone and was making sure she knew it.

"Alright, alright, shut up already," she muttered. She pushed the heavy oak door closed and threw her purse on the foyer table.

Sebastian sat on the stairs, looking at her. He wasn't happy.

"What?"

He bounded across the floor, stopped in front of her, and stared up at her. After a few seconds, he wagged his tail.

"I guess I'm forgiven." Cecily scooped him up and hugged him. He turned his face to look up at her, and she kissed him. He rested his head on her shoulder and sighed.

"You're spoiled rotten."

Sebastian grunted in response, so Cecily put him on the floor and headed for the kitchen, with the dog right on her heels. Once the spoiled Shih Tzu had a treat and she had a glass of water, she pulled her phone from her pocket. It had been on silent all night, and the reasons why stared her in the face.

First up, one missed call and a voicemail from her father. It was probably another phone call meant to chastise her for her choices in life—like breaking up with Lawrence or quitting her meaningless job with his company to pursue other interests. She wasn't in the mood to listen to it.

As usual, there were five missed calls from Lawrence, several text messages, and a voicemail. Just like every other day, but at least he was predictable. Six months after their breakup and he couldn't let go or wouldn't let go. Not that he was desperate to hold on to her out of love or even lust. His was an even more basic need.

Money.

Once upon a time, she thought Lawrence loved her. They met three months after she went to work for Devereaux Industries. Lawrence worked in accounting, while she worked as the company's overpaid party planner. She kept her familial relationships to herself to fit in with her co-workers and spent a lot of time hanging out with them—club-hopping, parties, late-night dinners. Lawrence was always there. He pursued her, intent on dating her. She found him to be quirky, attractive, and fun to be around, so they hit it off. Six months after they met, they were officially a couple.

Lawrence didn't know she was Claude Devereaux's daughter and the heir to the Devereaux's billion-dollar empire. At least Cecily thought he didn't know. When she told him, nine months after they started dating, he was unfazed and claimed he didn't care she was worth billions of dollars. He shrugged it off and told her money wasn't important to him.

Lawrence proposed on their one-year anniversary and of course, she accepted. Three months later things changed between them. His interest in her father's business intensified, and he sought out Claude to talk business regularly, both at work and when he was supposed to be spending time with her outside of work. Before she knew what happened, Lawrence was in line for a big promotion with Devereaux Industries, and her father couldn't stop singing her fiancé's praises. Lawrence pulled away from her, spending less time with her and more time with her father. He claimed he was "learning the ropes" of the business, but Cecily felt betrayed. He knew how contentious her relationship with Claude was, yet he didn't seem to care or want to help it.

His attitude toward her changed too. When they first started dating, he'd been doting and sweet, fawning over her. As his interest in Devereaux Industries increased, his attitude toward Cecily changed to where he ignored her phone calls and texts, made excuses to get out of lunch and dinner dates, and frequently commented unkindly on her looks and weight. It was so much like her father's attitude toward her that she began to wonder if Claude had somehow turned Lawrence against her.

The phone in her hand vibrated, yanking her out of her memories. Lawrence again. She hesitated for a minute before she hit the button and answered.

"I told you to stop calling me," she said instead of offering a greeting.

"CeCe! Thank God."

Cecily cringed, and her stomach rolled. "Don't call me that."

Lawrence sighed, and his voice took on that condescending tone she hated so much. "Cecily. I'm sorry. I'm just glad you answered. Can we talk?"

She perched on the edge of a kitchen chair, put her phone on speaker, and her head in her hands. "We are talking, Lawrence. What do you want?"

"Don't be like that."

"Like what? Irritated? Frustrated? Angry? Hurt? I don't think we have anything to talk about. You cheated; you lied; you're a shitty human being. See, nothing to talk about."

"We have a lot to talk about, honey—," Lawrence started to say before Cecily interrupted.

"I'm not your honey, Lawrence. I'm not anything to you, except maybe your ex-fiancée or, if that's too fancy for you, your ex-girlfriend. But I am not now, nor will I ever again be your honey." Cecily took a drink of her water. "Are we done?"

"I'm coming to Lakeside to see you," he explained.

"That's not a good idea—."

"We need to talk. Clear the air and set things right."

"We have nothing to talk about, Lawrence. I said everything I want to say to you six months ago. Stay in New York; I don't want you here." She ended the call and tossed her phone on the table.

It started ringing again. Cecily ignored it, shoved her chair away from the table, and got up. When was Lawrence going to get it through his thick head that she would not marry him? She contemplated calling him back and chewing him out, making it clear once and for all she wouldn't marry him. But it wasn't worth the headache.

Cecily whistled and patted her leg, getting her dog's attention. "Come on, Seb. Let's go to bed."

———

She woke up thinking about Lincoln. Knowing he was so close had her tingling all over, and she wondered if he'd call today.

Once the coffee was brewing, and Sebastian had taken several laps around the backyard, Cecily sat at the table with her phone in front of her. It rang, startling her. She checked the number on the screen before she reluctantly snatched it off the table. Might as well get it over with.

"Hello?" she answered.

"Cecily?"

"Hello, Daddy." She sat up, her shoulders back, and straightened the placemat under her coffee. "How are you?"

"I'm well." Her father cleared his throat. "You didn't return my call yesterday."

"I got in late last night and didn't want to wake you."

"Were you at that bar?" Her father's disdain was obvious even through the phone.

Cecily sighed. "Yes, I was at the Time Out bar. I like to hang out there. My friends are there."

"Perhaps you need better friends," her father suggested.

"I'm not having this argument with you again, Daddy." It was her turn to clear her throat. "I'm sure you called for a reason."

"You talked to Lawrence yesterday?" he asked.

He knows I did.

"I assume you talked to him too?"

"I did. You should sit down and discuss your issues with him. Give the boy a chance."

Her blood boiled. "I don't want to give him a chance, Daddy. I don't know why I need to keep saying this, but my relationship with Lawrence is between me and him. You have nothing to do with it. It's none of your business."

"I beg to differ. You are my daughter; therefore, it is my business. I like Lawrence—."

"Daddy."

"On second thought, maybe the three of us should talk. Sit down and talk it out."

"I don't want to—."

"You're acting like a petulant child, Cecily, and it's growing tiresome. You know what? I'm coming to Lakeside. We'll discuss the situation when I get to town. I'll let you know when I will be there. Don't even consider going anywhere; I expect you to be in Lakeside when I get there." The line disconnected.

"Nice talking to you too," she muttered to herself.

Dealing with her father was a nightmare, as his idea of a discussion was to guilt her to do what he wanted. Unfortunately, her father was on Lawrence's side and would do anything to get her to do what he wanted.

Claude Devereaux claimed to Cecily he was doing what was best for Devereaux Industries. He decided Lawrence was good for business, therefore Cecily marrying Lawrence was good for business. He considered it a business arrangement because love didn't matter, and what Cecily wanted didn't matter.

If only her mother were alive. Claude was much easier to handle when Deirdre Devereaux was alive because she kept him in check. Since her sudden death from a heart attack, Claude was impossible.

Cecily picked up her phone and squeezed it, as if she could somehow make it ring. She wanted Lincoln to call her, for he was a calm in the storm. Being with him and taking him to bed would help her forget her problems. She was determined to make it happen before her father and Lawrence arrived, a bit of fun before a lot of misery.

She pulled up a number from her contact list and hit the button. It only rang twice before the woman answered it.

"Cecily! Long time, no talk."

"Hey, Tia, I need a favor."

"Anything for you, you know that. Tell me what you need, and I'll make it happen."

Cecily grinned. "Let's start with one of your cabins."

Chapter 7

Cecily

By five o'clock on Saturday, just one day after seeing Lincoln, her plan was in place. Thank God she wasn't above taking matters into her own hands. Tia, owner of Stoner Creek Cabins, reserved the Stillwater cabin for the night for Cecily and promised to have it unlocked and ready as soon as she got Cecily's call. All she had to do was get Lincoln there.

After she fed Sebastian, she leaned against the kitchen counter and texted Lincoln.

[Cecily: Hey, heartbreaker. Are you free?]

It took less than thirty seconds to get an answer back.

[Lincoln: Yes, I am. Just finished helping
Serena and Van at the Ross's place.]

[Cecily: I want to see you. I know a place we can meet. I'll send you the address and directions.] You game?

[Lincoln: Absolutely.]

[Cecily: I'll meet you there in an hour.]

Cecily sent Lincoln the address, directions, and the cabin number. She got Sebastian settled in his room under the stairs, grabbed the bag she'd already packed, and left a note for her housekeeper and the island caretaker, Mr. and Mrs. Tuttle, to let them know she was out for the night.

She had hoped to get to the cabin first, but when she rounded the corner, she saw a truck parked next to the cabin and Lincoln leaning against it.

As she got out of the car, she grinned at him. "Hey."

"Hey, yourself," he replied. "Get your ass over here."

Cecily reached into the car, grabbed her bag, and followed Lincoln up a short set of stairs to the porch. Lincoln took her hand, intertwined his fingers with hers, and kissed her. Her heart skipped in her chest at the touch of his fingers against hers and the warmth of his lips on her skin. She tugged him toward the double doors leading inside. A shaky breath escaped her, as she sent up a silent prayer for strength. She was going to need it.

Cecily led Lincoln inside. The door swung shut behind them, and Lincoln was on her in an instant, his arms around her and his lips on hers, shoving his urgent and impatient tongue into her mouth.

She giggled but the sound was swallowed by Lincoln's mouth on hers. "Impatient much?" she mumbled.

"I can't resist you, sweetheart," Lincoln grumbled. "I need you." He yanked at the button on her jeans.

"Let's take a shower," she said. She took his hand and led him through the cabin to the bathroom down the hall.

Lincoln's lips never left her skin, even as she turned on the shower and stripped off her clothes. Once she was out of her clothes, she held Lincoln's head in her hands, kissing him as he yanked off his jeans and shirt.

Free of their clothes, Lincoln pushed her into the shower and shoved her against the tile wall. His body was flush against hers as steam billowed around them, the water falling over his broad shoulders and covering them.

Cecily ran her hands over his back and stomach, loving the feel of him. Last time they were together, it had been insane. The night went by so fast, she didn't have time to explore Lincoln's muscular body. Now she had the opportunity to memorize every inch of him—every scar, every mark—and she planned to take full advantage.

Lincoln moaned, the sound vibrating through his chest. Cecily continued her exploration, running her fingers over the taut muscles in his stomach and caressing his inner thighs. When she took his cock in her hand and stroked him, Lincoln's eyes rolled back in his head and a satisfied grunt escaped him. Cecily took her time brushing her thumb over the tip of his shaft with each upward swipe, drawing out his pleasure and savoring every one of Lincoln's gasping breaths as she ran her hand up and down his length.

After a few minutes, Lincoln grabbed her hands and held them over her head with one of his. He licked the water droplets from her neck and breasts, nipped at the sensitive skin beneath her ear, and rubbed his body against hers. Lincoln's hand drifted over her breasts, down her stomach, and between her legs. A smirk danced across his full, pink lips as his fingers teased at her entrance. He ducked his head and caught her lips in a kiss, a deep, soul-scorching kiss, distracting her as his fingers slipped inside her.

He released her, allowing her to take hold of him again. They moved in sync, moaning, gyrating, and grinding against each other. Lincoln's hips flexed as he thrust into Cecily's fist, while she pushed herself down on his long, thick fingers, trembling with every brush against her sweet spot.

"I want you to cum for me," Lincoln growled in her ear.

His words pushed her over the edge. Cecily gasped his name as she came, her walls clenching around his fingers. Her head fell back against the tile, and she squeezed her eyes closed as the sensations overtook her.

"I want you inside me, Lincoln," she whispered. "I *need* you inside me."

"Shit. We can't. Not now. I didn't bring a condom in here."

"It's okay. I'm on birth control. And I trust you." She squeezed his dick, twisting her hand at the last second, drawing a groan from him.

Lincoln's eyes closed, and he dragged in a shaky breath. "Fuck. Okay. I trust you too."

He slipped his arms around her, lifted her, and lowered her onto his throbbing shaft, filling her completely. He held her against the wall, legs spread, with one hand braced above her head and one arm still around her waist.

Cecily dragged her nails down his shoulders, leaving deep, red marks on his skin. He attacked her neck, biting and sucking, as he fucked her, his hips thrusting at a near maddening pace. She slid her hand down her stomach and between her legs, teasing herself as Lincoln's cock slipped in and out of her.

Lincoln growled, his voice wrecked with lust. "Jesus, sweetheart, that's fucking hot."

He slammed into her, his forehead pressed to hers and his cock buried deep inside her, pulsing as he came. Cecily dropped her head to his shoulder and gasped as her own climax rushed through her, sending her reeling with the onslaught of pleasure.

Lincoln set her on her feet, but he kept her in his arms, kissing her. They finished cleaning up and stepped out of the shower. He wrapped Cecily in a giant, fluffy towel, stopping every few seconds to kiss her cheek or shoulder.

Cecily dried her hair while Lincoln made drinks and checked out the cabin. When she was done, she found him in the bedroom, staring out the window at the lake through the trees, both drinks in his hands. She plucked her drink from his hand and sat cross-legged on the bed.

"Thanks for meeting me," she said. "I wasn't sure you would come, what with the wedding in a couple of days. You weren't busy?"

"I was, but I snuck away when I got a break."

"Won't Van be mad?" she asked.

Lincoln shrugged. "Maybe." He set his drink on the bedside table and crawled onto the bed. "But you're worth it." He tugged at her towel and pushed her down on the bed. He kissed her breasts and moved down her stomach until he hovered over her warm core.

Cecily giggled. "What are you doing? I thought we could have dessert. Tia put something in the fridge."

"You're my dessert." He pushed open her thighs and settled himself between her legs.

The first touch of his tongue caused a delicious tightening of the muscles in her stomach and a satisfied sigh to slip past her lips. When his mouth closed over her, she couldn't hold back a scream of pleasure, nor could she stop the obscene noises she made as he repeatedly brought her to orgasm. By the time he pulled away, she was shaking and breathless.

Lincoln rolled her to her stomach and entered her from behind, thrusting hard and deep. Cecily pushed back against him and took every inch of his substantial length, the pillow under her head swallowing her screams.

They collapsed to the bed, limbs tangled together, face to face. Lincoln tucked her hair behind her ear and pressed a kiss to her forehead. She fell asleep beside him soon after, his hand on her waist and hers on his chest.

Cecily woke three hours later, the blankets on the bed covering her nakedness. Lincoln laid on his stomach, his arms wrapped around the pillow under his head, as light snores came from him. After checking the clock on the bedside table, she grabbed her bag from the floor and quickly dressed; it was much later than she thought. She jotted a note on the pad by the phone and dropped it on the pillow by Lincoln's head.

Cecily paused at the door and looked back over her shoulder at him. She knew she would see him in a couple of days at Van and Serena's wedding, but she liked this look on him, satisfied and sleepy. Maybe they could get another round or two in before he went back to New York; that should be enough to get him out of her system.

She sighed. If only her life wasn't so complicated, things could be different between them. But Devereaux Industries would always and forever stand between her and love. She would always wonder if any man who professed to love her actually loved her or was more interested in her for her connection to one of the most powerful companies in the world. It was the reason she hadn't told Lincoln who her father was.

The news would taint what they had, and what they had was damn near perfect. Walking away while things were good would be the wise thing to do, and her heart would stay intact.

"See you later, handsome," she murmured. She pulled the door closed and left.

Chapter 8

Lincoln

The ceremony was over, Mason, the wedding photographer, had taken the wedding photos, and the DJ had introduced the newlyweds as husband and wife to the waiting crowd. It was time to mingle while they waited for dinner to be served. Lincoln found Van's mom and sister and spent a few minutes talking with them before excusing himself to search for the open bar. He needed a minute, a stiff drink and to catch his breath; it had been a long day.

Lincoln had been up before the sun, joining Van in a run along the lake. They used to run through Central Park before going to work, but it had been a long time ago. It was a relief to see Van working out and taking care of himself, better than the days after Adelaide's death when he drank himself to oblivion and barely slept. Though Lincoln grumbled when Van dragged him out of bed, he had to admit the run and the fresh Montana air rejuvenated him.

Good thing too, because it had been nonstop madness for the last twelve hours. But the wedding was over, and the party had started, so Lincoln wanted to kick back and have some fun, which would start with a stiff drink.

While he waited for the bartender, he pulled his phone from his pocket to see if Cecily texted him back. He didn't know whether they invited her to the wedding or not. He tried to look for her during the ceremony, but the sun shone in his eyes standing at the altar and he could not see past the first row of seats.

Lincoln couldn't get Cecily off his mind. The last two nights, he fell asleep with the image of her in his head. It annoyed him when he woke up at the cabin and she was gone, but part of him understood; staying overnight was a step toward commitment and feelings. He got the impression Cecily was about as uninterested in a relationship as he was, though spending more time with her appealed to him. He was sure it would get her out of his system before he left.

Lincoln put his phone in his pocket. He'd spend a few minutes looking for her, but if he couldn't find her, he'd get drunk and have fun at his best friend's wedding.

Charlie Ross, Serena's boss and the owner of the home they currently partied in, clapped him on the back and leaned against the bar beside him.

"Van tells me you need a job."

Lincoln burst out laughing. "I hate to be the one to break it to you, Mr. Ross, but I don't need a job. Van is looking for a way to get me to move out here."

Ross chuckled. "Please, call me Charlie. I'll tell you what, if you ever need a job, I'd love to bring you on at the university. Van tells me you have an extensive background in security consulting. We could use someone like you at the university."

"You have Van," Lincoln said. "He's the one who's good with all that stuff."

"According to him, you're better. I would love to have both of you working for me."

"A crack team of two?"

"Yep." Charlie laughed. "Think about it. If you guys ran Lakeside College's security, I wouldn't have anything to worry about. Nothing."

Lincoln smiled. "I'll keep it on the back burner. Now, if you'll excuse me, I'm trying to find a friend." He picked up his drink, thanked the bartender, and wandered back through the house.

He was almost back outside when he spotted a voluptuous, gorgeous body wrapped in an emerald-green dress twenty feet in front of him. A black braid hung down her bare back, swinging between her shoulder blades. He recognized the swing of those hips.

"Cecily!"

She froze, turned around slowly with her hands on her hips, and gave him a sexy smile. "Lincoln. I've been looking for you."

He reached out and caressed her arm. She stepped closer to him and kissed his cheek, lingering with her hand pressed to his chest. The smell of orange blossoms filled his head.

"You smell delicious," he whispered. His lips brushed the shell of her ear, and she shivered.

Cecily laughed. "You are insatiable, aren't you?"

"Only when I'm with you, sweetheart." He took her hand. "I wasn't sure if you were here or not."

"Serena and I are friends. I work part-time at the college for her boss, Charlie. We've gotten to know each other working together the last six months. She's sweet; Van's a lucky man."

"Yes, he is." He leaned over her. "What are you doing later? Van and Serena are staying in Charlie's guest house tonight, and I have the condo to myself. You should come over. I believe I owe you dessert."

Cecily sighed. "God, I wish I could." Her face pinched like she was sucking on a lemon.

"What's wrong?"

Cecily glanced around at the people hanging around the bar before she spoke. "Nothing. I'm fine."

Her pinched face and furrowed brow told Lincoln she was lying. Something or someone had upset her. He sighed, took her arm, and steered her through the house, looking for an empty room. He spotted an open door, pulled Cecily inside what looked to be an office, and pushed the door closed.

"Okay, we're alone." Lincoln crossed his arms over his chest and stared her down. "Tell me what's wrong."

Cecily snorted and shook her head. "I told you, it's nothing." She spun on her heel, stalked across the room, and stopped a few feet from the window. She wrapped her arms around herself and shivered.

Lincoln followed her, stopping a foot behind her. "You're a lousy liar, Cecily. It's obvious that something is wrong. What is it?"

Cecily laughed ruefully and shook her head. "I am a lousy liar." She smoothed the front of her dress. "I'm expecting company later this week, my father and, I assume, my ex-fiancé. I am not looking forward to it. It's bugging me enough that it shows on my face; I'm not good at hiding my emotions. Right now, I am in a bad place and doubt I'd be much fun."

"Do you want to talk about it?"

Cecily huffed. "No, not really."

Lincoln moved closer and rested his hand on the small of her back. "Okay, we won't talk about it. How about you forget about whoever is coming to visit? I know that's a lot to ask, but I'm asking, anyway. Let's go have a good time celebrating my best friend and his wife. We'll drink, party, and forget about everyone else."

Cecily turned around and grinned at him. "How do you see this evening ending? Both of us drunk and passed out somewhere?"

"God, I hope not." He took her arm and spun her in a circle, twirling her around until he ensconced her in his arms. He pushed her against the window, took her chin in his hand, and kissed her. When they broke apart, they were both panting. "I'd like the evening to stretch into morning. In fact, I'll be in Lakeside for the next two weeks on vacation" Lincoln slid his hand down her back and cupped her ass. "We can spend the next two weeks drowning in each other, and when it's over, we can part as friends, lovers, or we can forget the other person exists. But let's make the next two weeks worthwhile." His lips drifted down the side of her neck as he lightly kissed her.

Cecily moaned, and her head fell slightly against the window. She gripped Lincoln's shoulders tight. "Two weeks?" she asked. "Then we walk away, no hard feelings if one of us doesn't want more?"

"Two weeks, Cecily. What do you say?"

Cecily nodded, wrapped her hand around the back of his neck, and pulled him in for a kiss.

"I think it sounds like a fabulous fucking idea."

———

Lincoln dropped his fork on the table and picked up his drink. He signaled one of the wait staff to bring him another one, then he leaned back in his chair and smiled at Cecily.

"So, how long have you lived in Lakeside?" Lincoln asked.

Cecily tapped her chin. "Off and on for years. At first, it was just summers. When I was in junior high—I guess I must have been about thirteen or fourteen—my mom tired of moving all the time because of my father's business. She decided that the two of us would come live here so I could go to school. Mom wanted me in public school, making friends and living a normal teenage life. Daddy suggested boarding school, but Mom was adamant we come here. She didn't want to be away from me. We stayed until I graduated from high school and left for college. After I left, she moved to New York with my father. They kept the house, and I spent most of my summers in Lakeside. Six months ago, I moved here for good."

"So, you graduated from high school here?"

"Lakeside Unified, grades seven through twelve. I can tell you, being the new kid in a school where the other students have known each other since kindergarten isn't easy. Being the rich kid compounds those problems."

Lincoln raised an eyebrow. "The rich kid?" Maybe it was the alcohol or maybe she was finally comfortable with him, but it pleased him that she was sharing with him.

Cecily signed and nodded. "I guess I didn't mention that my father is worth a lot—it's more like a substantial amount—of money. It made things difficult growing up." She didn't elaborate, and he didn't press. She would tell him when she was ready. "I was also a bookworm and painfully shy. I was fat, at least according to the girls in school."

Lincoln pursed his lips. "Kids are jerks."

Cecily laughed. "You're not wrong. They are jerks, especially when you don't fit the mold. I wasn't athletic, I didn't ride horses, or hang out with everybody at the lake. I was used to being alone or being the only kid around a bunch of adults. At a young age, I learned to entertain myself. I was happy to stay home and read my books. I liked to study, and yes, I was overweight. Not fat, per se, but I was heavier than most girls my age. Kids don't know how to handle people who aren't like them. They don't understand, and they don't want to take the time to understand. It's not until they're older that they learn to be tolerant of people who aren't like them." She made a face like she'd sucked on a lemon or a sour grape. "Or at least you hope they do."

Lincoln caressed her arm. "I'm sorry. People are assholes."

"It was a long time ago," Cecily said. "I'm over it."

Lincoln narrowed his eyes. "It doesn't seem like it. You're not still bothered by a bunch of teenage jerks, are you?"

Cecily laughed. "No. Now I'm bothered by the adult jerks in my life: Lawrence Bronson and Claude Devereaux."

"Claude Devereaux? You know Claude Devereaux of Devereaux Industries?"

Cecily snorted. "I'd say so. He is my father."

"Wait a minute." Lincoln's heart thumped in his chest, and he had to swallow back a groan of frustration. "You're Claude Devereaux's daughter?"

Shit.

Cecily cleared her throat. "I am. I take it you've heard of my father?"

"Who hasn't? He's one of the richest men in the world, in the news and tabloids all the time. I can't believe—." His mouth snapped shut.

"You can't believe what?"

"I just ... I can't believe you're his daughter. I've never seen *you* in the news or the tabloids."

"My parents were extremely careful about keeping me out of the spotlight. And I don't make a habit of telling people I'm his daughter. Too many complications."

"I can imagine," Lincoln mumbled.

After the way he'd ended his business arrangement with Devereaux, Cecily Devereaux was the last person on earth he should be involved with. He opened his mouth to tell her as much and tell her he knew her father—had in fact worked for him—but the music cut out and the DJ called for the crowd's attention. Lincoln scrubbed a hand over the back of his neck; it was time for his speech.

He downed his drink and dropped his glass to the table. He'd tell Cecily later when he wasn't making speeches and a bunch of people able to eavesdrop on their conversation surrounded them. Instead, he leaned over her, wrapped a hand around the back of her neck, and tugged her close. He pressed his lips to her ear. "When this night is over, you're coming back to my place, and I'm going to make you forget all about your troubles. Sound good?"

Cecily sighed. "That sounds amazing."

Lincoln kissed the shell of her ear and got to his feet. Cecily smiled up at him, so he couldn't resist bending over and kissing her again. She giggled and pushed him away, mouthing "go" at him. Reluctantly, he turned back to the stage. He could listen to her laugh all day and all night. At least she was smiling.

I'll do anything to keep that smile on her face. Anything.

Chapter 9

Cecily

"Come home with me."

When Lincoln purred those words in her ear just after midnight, she melted. *How could she resist?* That deep, sexy, blow-her-clothes-off-with-one-word voice was why she was in his bed, snuggled under his arm and half asleep. Before they dozed off, he made her promise she wouldn't sneak off, as he wanted to wake up next to her.

They had the condo to themselves. Van and Serena were on their way to Glacier for the next week with their dog in tow. Lincoln told her he planned to stay in Montana not only to babysit Van and Serena's two condos, but because he needed a vacation, and Lakeside was the perfect place to escape the madness of New York City.

The next morning, Cecily didn't wake up with Lincoln; to her surprise, she woke up alone, buried under a pile of blankets. She sat up, stretched, and checked the clock. It was early, not even eight. Noises came from the kitchen, noises that sounded a lot like someone cooking. Cecily crawled out of bed, pulled the down comforter around herself, and followed the sounds.

"Hey, gorgeous," Lincoln said. "How did you sleep?"

"Um, I actually slept well," she replied. "What are you doing?"

"Making you breakfast. There's a T-shirt and a pair of my sweats in the bathroom. They might be a little big, but you're welcome to them. I thought that might be more comfortable than your party dress."

"Toothbrush?"

"Extra one in the bathroom next to the clothes. Hurry, though. The food will be ready in a few minutes."

Cecily made her way down the hall to the bathroom and closed herself inside. She dropped the comforter to the floor and grabbed Lincoln's shirt and sweats. They were more than a little big; they were huge, but not uncomfortable. She brushed her teeth and smoothed her hair, then she returned to the kitchen and sat at the table.

Lincoln kissed the top of her head and set a plate in front of her of eggs, bacon, and toast.

Jesus, he cooks too? Damn it, why is he so perfect?

"Do you want coffee, tea, milk, or orange juice? I've got all of them."

"How about a glass of orange juice?"

Lincoln poured her a glass, then he sat next to her with his own plate of food. He was a hearty eater, devouring several eggs, bacon, and two pieces of toast in short order. He belched quietly and grinned at her.

Cecily laughed. "Were you hungry?"

"Good sex makes me hungry." He winked at her.

"You're incorrigible," she mumbled.

"I know." He cleared the plates off the table and dumped them in the sink. "What are your plans for the day?"

She sighed. "I need to go home, let my dog out, and get ready for my company." She rolled her eyes. "Getting my head in the right place takes time."

Lincoln leaned against the counter and crossed his arms. "Tell me about your company."

"Trust me, you don't want to know." She sipped her juice.

"Sure, I do. Tell me."

Cecily snorted. "Okay, but it's a mess. Remember, you asked." She took a deep breath and exhaled before she spoke. "My father is coming to town. And I have a sneaking suspicion my ex-fiancé Lawrence will be with him."

Lincoln narrowed his eyes. "Why?"

Cecily shrugged. "A hunch. My father might be a savvy businessman, but with me, he's predictable to a fault. He'll bring Lawrence with him."

"Why would he do that to you?"

"Because Daddy thinks I should have married Lawrence. He desperately wanted me to marry him. Daddy *likes* Lawrence—scratch that—Daddy loves Lawrence. My father has plans for him, and I ruined those plans by breaking off the engagement. He is extremely upset with me for ending the relationship."

"You obviously had a reason for doing it."

She nodded. "I did." She narrowed her eyes. "Are you sure you want to hear this?"

"I wouldn't have asked if I didn't."

Cecily sighed. Recounting her past with Lawrence made her queasy. "Lawrence is a jerk. When we first started dating, he seemed sweet and attentive. Looking back, I realize I ignored a lot of stupid stuff he did and said. I think at the time my feelings blinded me."

Lincoln nodded. "I get it. Love is blind. We don't see what people are really like until it's too late."

Cecily tipped her head and narrowed her eyes. This was the first time Lincoln had hinted at any previous relationship. *What does he mean when he says he gets it?*

Lincoln didn't offer any additional information, so Cecily continued. "I hid who I was for a long time and when I finally told him I was Claude Devereaux's daughter, it didn't go as I expected."

"Were there complications with Lawrence?"

Cecily shook her head. "No. It was weird. He didn't seem surprised, and he claimed he didn't care who my father was or that I was the heir to a billion-dollar empire. It sealed the deal; I agreed to marry him. But once we got engaged, he changed. Suddenly, everything in Lawrence's life was about my father and Devereaux Industries. It didn't take long to realize he didn't love me; he loved my father's money and the idea of being in control of that money."

Lincoln raised an eyebrow. "Oh?"

"I guess Daddy promised him a big promotion or something after we were married. I was nothing more than a means to an end, but I'm better than that. I'm not someone's meal ticket. I broke off the engagement and moved out here. My father has been on my case ever since."

"Jesus, Cecily. He sounds like a real ass."

"Lawrence or my father?"

Lincoln grunted. "Both."

"You're not wrong." Cecily pinched the bridge of her nose. "You know what? I don't want to talk about it anymore. This whole thing is a colossal pain in my neck."

Lincoln shrugged. "Okay." He grinned at her. "Let's talk about something else. Can you stay for a while?"

She laughed. "I think I can stay a little longer." Her voice dropped to a conspiratorial whisper. "But only if I can get you to take me back to bed."

"Sounds like a plan to me," Lincoln said. He grabbed her, pulled her out of the chair, and kissed her all the way to the bedroom.

———

Sebastian was all over her when she arrived home. She felt bad leaving him home all night for the second time that week, but it wasn't like he had been alone. Mr. and Mrs. Tuttle were more than happy to take care of him. Not that Sebastian was happy about it. The second Cecily came through the door, he was under her feet and following her everywhere, even into the bathroom. He brought her toy after toy, barking at her until she tossed them across the room. It took almost an hour to wear him out.

She was on her way to take a shower when her phone rang; it was her father. She sat down at the top of the stairs and answered her phone. Sensing her tension, Sebastian curled up in her lap.

"Hi, Daddy."

"I'll be there on Thursday," her father said.

"Hello to you too," she mumbled.

"Cecily, I don't have time for your nonsense. We'll be in Kalispell in the morning and at the house two hours later. Have Mrs. Tuttle get my room ready. I will see you on Thursday." The phone disconnected.

Cecily pushed herself to her feet, tucked Sebastian under one arm, and went to find Mrs. Tuttle. She informed the housekeeper that her father would arrive on Thursday, to which Mrs. Tuttle promised to have his room ready. Confident Lawrence would be with her father, she suggested Mrs. Tuttle get one of the guest rooms made up as well. Cecily encouraged her to prepare one on the opposite side of the house from her room. The further away from her, the better.

Cecily took a quick shower, grabbed a book from her room, a pitcher of Mrs. Tuttle's fresh lemonade, and went out onto the patio. After her romp with Lincoln, she was tired. Within a half hour, she was asleep on the lounge chair, with Sebastian next to her.

If her cellphone had stayed quiet, she would have slept for hours. Instead, it rang incessantly, pulling her from a pleasant dream about Lincoln. She snatched the phone off the table where she'd left it and answered it without looking at the number.

"Hello?"

"Let's go out to dinner Thursday night," Lawrence said. "I'm sure there's someplace decent in Kalispell."

Christ. Seriously?

She scrubbed a hand over her face. She wasn't awake enough for this conversation. "I don't want to go to dinner with you, Lawrence. Besides, how do you know I don't have plans?"

"Plans? With whom? Those friends of yours at the bar? I'm sure you can cancel any plans you have with them."

Cecily squeezed her cellphone so tight, she heard the case squeak. "It's not with my friends from the bar," she blurted. "I have a date. For your information, I've been seeing someone."

She didn't know why she said it or why it came out of her mouth so easily; it was a lie.

Not really. I have been seeing someone. I see him every time we have sex.

Lawrence seethed; she could hear it through the phone, the sharp, repeated intakes of breath and the smacking of his lips. She'd grown accustomed to those sounds when they'd dated. After thirty seconds of silence, he cleared his throat. "You're seeing someone."

It wasn't a question; it was her chance to back out of it, to correct herself; it was her chance to tell him she wasn't really seeing someone, and they were only friends. Instead, she said, "Yes, that's what I said. His name is Lincoln, and we've been seeing each other for about three months."

And just like that, it was out there, and she couldn't take it back. Cecily rubbed the center of her forehead.

What did I just do?

Lawrence huffed. "Well, I can't wait to meet him. I'm sure your father would like to meet him as well. I'll tell him you have a new boyfriend when we fly in. See you Thursday, CeCe."

The line disconnected.

"Shit!"

Sebastian grunted, opened one eye, and stared at her, annoyed she woke him up. He jumped off the chaise lounge, made his way across the yard to plop down beneath one of the lilac bushes, and promptly went back to sleep.

"Yeah, buddy, join the club. I'm annoyed with me too."

Cecily put her head in her hands and rubbed her temples with her thumbs.

Holy hell. What am I going to do?

Chapter 10

Lincoln

Cecily's panicked phone call forced him off the couch, away from the ballgame, and into action. When he'd last seen her Tuesday morning, she was fine. She was wary of her father's visit but wasn't the desperate woman who called him now. A lot changed in twenty-four hours, and she begged him to meet her at the Time Out Bar and Grill because she needed to talk to him right away. He promised to be there in ten minutes.

Lincoln parked in the lot's corner and jumped from the truck. He strode quickly through the parking lot and, once inside, his eyes darted around, taking in everything. Cecily was at the bar, a little white dog with brown spots curled up by her feet and a drink in her hand. She looked as if she'd lost her best friend. He pushed through the crowd and stopped beside her, his hand on her back.

"Are you okay?" he asked.

Cecily finished her drink, dropped the glass to the bar, and shook her head.

"No."

Lincoln eased into the seat beside her. The dog looked up at him and yipped before putting his head on his paws and staring up at Lincoln, like he was assessing his character.

"Who's your little friend?"

"That's Sebastian. He's all bark and no bite, trust me. He's just making sure you know he's here."

Lincoln held out his hand so the dog could smell it. Sebastian rose to his feet and sniffed Lincoln's fingers. Apparently satisfied with what he smelled, he huffed and laid down. Lincoln turned his attention back to Cecily.

"Okay, what's wrong? You've got me worried."

"I screwed up, Lincoln. Big time."

He gestured to the bartender, pointed at Cecily's empty glass, and held up two fingers. Drinks ordered, he turned back to Cecily.

"What did you do?"

She grabbed his hand and squeezed it. "I need to ask you a huge favor, Lincoln. And when I say huge, I mean huge. I'm begging you to say yes."

He narrowed his eyes and sat up straight, his shoulders back. He cleared his throat and rubbed the center of his forehead. Huge favors never ended well for him.

"Tell me what you need, and then I'll decide whether I'll say yes." The bartender, his name tag said Andy, set their drinks down, took one look at Cecily's face, and scurried away.

Cecily gave him a weak smile. "I guess I shouldn't assume you'll do it just because we're having sex, should I?"

Lincoln chuckled and shrugged. "Never assume, but I didn't say I wouldn't help. Tell me what you need, Cecily." He took a sip of his drink.

"I want you to be my boyfriend."

Lincoln sputtered and choked on his drink. He wiped his mouth with the back of his hand and stared at Cecily.

"I'm ... I'm sorry, what?"

Cecily laughed, a hollow, twittering gasp that sounded like a choking bird. "I know how it sounds. I do, and I swear I'm not suddenly in dire need of a relationship. Jesus, that's the last thing I need." She exhaled. "Okay, let me try to explain." She twisted a napkin around her fingers and stared at it instead of looking at him. "Lawrence *is* coming with my father."

"Okay." Lincoln drew the word out. "What does that have to do with me?"

"I might have told him you're my boyfriend." She put her face in her hands and burst out laughing. "Oh my God, I'm so sorry." She scrubbed her face, straightened her shoulders, and turned to face him. A tear slid down her cheek, and she absentmindedly wiped it away.

Lincoln took her hand and intertwined his fingers with hers. "Don't apologize." This wasn't the woman he knew. Normally, she exuded a confidence he admired. She always knew what she wanted and how she would get it. However, this wasn't the Cecily who swept *him* off his feet and took him into her bed.

She gave him a weak smile. "I feel like an idiot. I shouldn't have said anything to Lawrence, but he sets me on edge. It just came out, you know. He wanted to go to dinner and talk about us. I got sick of being bombarded with his stupid requests to talk about *us,* so I blurted out that I had a boyfriend." She shrugged. "Now I need one."

"Cecily—."

"You know what? Forget I said anything. I'll figure something out."

What is wrong with me? She's asking for help.

"I'll do it," Lincoln said.

"Seriously?"

"Yes, seriously."

Cecily threw her arms around his neck. "You're the best, Lincoln. I mean it, the best. I owe you."

Lincoln hugged her close and pressed his mouth to her ear. "Trust me, sweetheart. I plan on collecting that debt."

———

They moved to a booth in the back corner of the bar, ordered food, and a pitcher of beer. Now would be the perfect time to confess to Cecily that not only did he know her father, but he'd worked for him as well. Just because they were going to lie to other people about the reality of their so-called relationship didn't mean they should lie to each other.

He was about to tell her but then their server, Trista, appeared with their order. She also brought Sebastian a cut-up hamburger, a dish of water, and a small squeaky toy. Sebastian jumped around the booth and onto the floor, desperate to get his paws on the toy. Cecily took the toy and spent a few minutes tossing it around for Sebastian before she returned to the table. Sebastian jumped onto the seat and set to work devouring his hamburger.

Cecily poured their beers, picked up an onion ring, and nibbled on it. "You're really okay with this?" she asked.

Lincoln took a healthy swallow of his beer, leaned back in the booth, and smiled at Cecily. "Alright, let's talk details."

"Details?"

"It would help if we got our stories straight. How we met, where, when we met, how long we've been dating, that kind of thing."

Cecily pushed a hand through her hair and shifted in her seat. "Maybe this was a bad idea; it's too complicated. I'm not a talented liar."

"It doesn't have to be complicated, and you won't have to tell too many lies." Lincoln tapped his fingers on the tabletop. "We shadow the lies in the truth."

"What do you mean?"

"We tell the truth, or at least most of the truth, about how we met. In New York, three months ago, at a bar. We hit it off and dated." Lincoln shrugged. "The lie mixed with the truth."

Cecily munched on an onion ring. "You make it sound so easy." She narrowed her eyes and looked him up and down. "Why are you so agreeable about this whole thing? You didn't have to say yes. You could have told me to shove it."

"Where's the fun in that, babe?"

Cecily giggled and shook her head. "You're incorrigible."

Lincoln winked. "I know."

—

He threw himself on the bed, his arm over his eyes.
What the hell am I doing?

Agreeing to pretend to be Cecily's boyfriend was a bad idea. It meant spending a lot of time together while her father was here. He still hadn't told her he had worked for her father, a secret he would not keep much longer. Once Claude Devereaux saw him, the cat would be out of the bag. He and Claude had parted ways less than amicably; in fact, it had been damn near an all-out war once Lincoln confronted Devereaux about his nefarious business dealings.

At first, Claude shrugged it off, claiming it was no big deal and he could walk away any time he chose. Lincoln knew that wasn't the case, especially given the people he'd gotten himself tangled up with. He tried to explain that to Claude, but the stubborn businessman thought he knew best and refused to listen. When Lincoln explained he would no longer be working for Devereaux Industries because of his business associates, Devereaux had exploded, vowing to destroy Lincoln's business and reputation if he quit.

It had taken all his self-control not to let loose on Devereaux. He explained that Brooks and Dunn Security would no longer work for Claude's company. Then he walked out of the building and straight to the bar, where he met Cecily.

But there was more to it than the massive lie of omission hanging over his head. He felt an overwhelming attachment to Cecily that he did not want to feel. Acting like her fake boyfriend would make it a lot harder to walk away from her. He contemplated picking up the phone, calling her, and telling her he changed his mind. Except he couldn't stop thinking about the look on her face, the pain and even fear.

Lincoln sat up and scrubbed a hand over his face. This was stupid. He didn't get attached; he didn't get involved. After Cat, he put all that behind him.

Catherine Crowley was Lincoln's high school sweetheart and ex-wife. They'd married right out of high school, six weeks before he and Van left for boot camp. They were deeply in love, or so he thought.

After boot camp, the army whisked him away for additional training and then sent him to Afghanistan. He didn't get to see Cat before he left, something he always regretted. They kept in touch via snail mail, email, and infrequent phone calls. As time went on, Cat pulled away. The letters stopped, and the emails dwindled to once every week or two until they eventually stopped altogether. Lincoln brushed it off as a wife's fear and difficulty of being married to a military man.

When he could finally go home between his first and second tour, it seemed like a good idea to surprise the wife he hadn't seen in nine months. He'd gone straight to their small apartment from the airport, unlocked his front door, and walked into his home that was filled with another man's belongings. He was the surprised one. His entire world, his entire belief system, and his faith in love conquering all disintegrated on the spot. Cat served him with divorce papers two days later. She married Todd, her boss and new boyfriend, two months after the divorce was final.

Lincoln vowed to never fall in love again. The heartbreak Van suffered after his wife's death only solidified his decision. Love was messy, complicated, and not worth the heartache. Avoiding any kind of long-term relationship was easy; any time a girl got too close or too clingy, he walked away. Most of the time, he didn't stick around long enough to get to the clingy stage. Van teased him about being a one-and-done-kind of guy, which was a reputation Lincoln welcomed.

"Nine days until I'm gone. I'll put Cecily Devereaux behind me and get on with my life," he said out loud. Hearing the words made it seem more definitive. He would help her out of this jam, then go back to New York and back to his life of no emotional commitments and no heartache.

"Easy peasy," he mumbled.

Chapter 11

Cecily

Cecily paced the back patio with Sebastian at her feet. She checked her watch every few minutes, eager to get past the mundane and tedious greetings accompanying a visit with her father. They were embarrassingly awkward with each other, almost like they weren't related.

It was worse after her mother passed away. Once she was gone, Cecily and her father had nothing in common and nothing to talk about. Her father's focus shifted to getting her married off to an appropriate suitor, wanting to pawn her and the problems she caused him off on someone else.

Every few seconds, she glanced across the lake, but she didn't see the boat crossing the water. She grabbed a glass of lemonade off the patio table and chugged half of it, then wiped the back of her hand across her mouth.

I will not survive this.

Since the phone call with Lawrence and her meeting with Lincoln, she'd teetered on the edge of a nervous breakdown. Fear twisted her stomach into knots: fear of getting caught in a lie, of disappointing her father, of screwing up and giving into her father's demands. It had always been difficult to stand up to him, more difficult than she would admit out loud. If he pressured her to reconcile with Lawrence, she feared she might give in to his demands.

The roar of a speedboat's engine caught her attention. Cecily pushed a hand through her hair and squared her shoulders.

Here we go.

Her father was at the helm, their caretaker in the passenger seat, and Lawrence was in the middle of the boat, ensconced in a large life jacket with a death grip on the edge of his seat. Her ex-fiancé hated large bodies of water— the ocean, lakes, even large rivers. He had never visited the home on the lake, especially after he discovered it was on an island three miles offshore. Cecily tried many times to get him to visit her home in Montana, but he always refused.

If he will come all the way out here, he must be desperate to look good for my father.

Cecily raised her hand and waved. Claude Devereaux returned the wave, but Lawrence maintained his hold on the boat. She picked up Sebastian, pressed a kiss to the top of his head as she attached his leash to his harness, and wrapped it around her wrist. She then stepped through the recently installed gate, put in to keep Sebastian from running off. He liked to take off into the woods surrounding the house, so she never let him outside the gate without his leash, even if she carried him.

As she made her way down the path to the dock, she watched Claude pull the boat alongside the floating wood, jump out, and secure the line to the moor. Lawrence didn't move until her father completed his tasks.

"Cecily." Her father kissed her cheek and gave Sebastian a cursory pat on his head. The dog allowed it, even though Cecily knew he didn't like her father.

Lawrence climbed off the boat and stumbled over a raised board on the dock, the too-large life jacket hitting him in the chin. He pushed his glasses up his nose and plastered one of his fake smiles on his face.

"CeCe, love! It's so good to see you." He descended on her, his hands outstretched as he leaned in to kiss her.

Sebastian snarled and nipped at Lawrence, catching the corner of the life jacket between his teeth. He tugged on it and growled.

"Sebastian, no," Cecily said half-heartedly.

The dog looked up at her, but he released Lawrence with one of his irritated huffs. Cecily took a step back, avoiding Lawrence's damp lips, and smiled at him.

"Lawrence," she said. She turned to her father. "How was the flight, Daddy?"

"Bumpy," he grumbled. "Let's get up to the house. I could use a drink."

Cecily nodded and followed her father up the dock. Lawrence paused long enough to remove the life jacket and toss it in the boat before joining them. Mr. Tuttle followed them, two suitcases in his hands.

Once they reached the lawn, Cecily set Sebastian on the ground, removed his leash, and pulled the gate closed behind her father and Lawrence.

"The fencing looks good, Cecily," her father commented. "Did Will do it?"

"Yes, sir. All I ask is that you remember to keep the gate closed; otherwise, Sebastian gets out and heads straight for the water or into the woods. I don't want him to get hurt, so please keep it shut."

Lawrence snorted. "You put a fence around the back patio to keep your dog in? Isn't that a little excessive? Why not keep him inside?"

"He likes to play outside," Cecily said.

"We will keep the gate closed," Claude interjected. "I know how much you like that little dog. Now, let's get that drink before we go to dinner. My secretary made us reservations at The Montana Club."

Cecily headed for her father's office, with Sebastian at her feet, while Claude and Lawrence settled themselves up in their rooms. Lawrence came down first and walked right up to Cecily. Sebastian growled at him as Lawrence passed the dog. Her ex took her arm, dragged her close, and pressed a damp kiss to her cheek.

"I missed you," he whispered.

She yanked her arm free and stepped back until there were several feet between them. "No, you missed my father's money and the prospect of a promotion in the company."

"Don't be like that," Lawrence muttered. "I *missed* you. We should sit down and talk, see if we can work something out."

"I don't want to work anything out, Lawrence, because I don't want to get back together. Marrying you is no longer in my best interests. When we broke up, I thought I made that clear. And every time we talked every day for the last six months."

Lawrence sucked on his bottom lip. "Do you think you can do better than me? Look at you, CeCe. You haven't changed. You're still overweight—."

"I'm fine the way I am," she snapped.

"You've put on a lot of weight."

Cecily pinched the bridge of her nose. "I'm not having this discussion with you, not again. This is one reason we aren't together anymore. You made it perfectly clear how you felt about my weight gain. Obviously, you haven't moved past it."

Claude entered the study. "Moved past what?" he asked.

"Nothing, Daddy. It's not important." Cecily moved to the other side of the room and sat on the recliner. Sebastian followed her and sat beside her, with his head resting on her calf.

Claude raised an eyebrow, but he chose not to comment. He made himself a drink, then he sat behind his enormous mahogany desk. He leaned back in his chair and crossed his arms.

Cecily mirrored her father, crossing her arms as she leaned back. Two could play his game.

"Lawrence tells me you've been dating someone," Claude stated. "Invite him to dinner tonight. I'd like to meet him."

She opened her mouth and closed it again; there was no sense in arguing with her father. Besides, she and Lincoln planned for this. Putting off the meeting wouldn't do any good; it would get Lawrence out of her hair too.

"I'll call him and have him meet us there." She shoved herself to her feet. "I'm going to get ready. Come on, Sebby, let's go."

The Shih Tzu got up and followed her, giving both her father and Lawrence a wide berth. Cecily pulled her phone from her pocket and dialed Lincoln's number. He picked up on the first ring.

"Showtime," she whispered.

———

Cecily watched the restaurant door, half-listening to her father and Lawrence talk. Lincoln was late.

"I'll make the arrangements." Claude cleared his throat. "Cecily? You are available, aren't you?"

Cecily dragged her gaze away from the door and turned her attention to her father. "I'm sorry, available for what?"

"To come back to New York with us. You have had enough fun in Lakeside; it's time to come back to New York and resume your job with Devereaux Industries." Her father jutted a finger in Lawrence's direction. "Also, we need to discuss your ridiculous decision to break off your engagement to Lawrence."

Cecily shook her head about her father and his impossible demands. She exhaled and started with the job. "You mean my meaningless job as the company party-planner? That job?"

"It's not meaningless—."

"My master's degree is in business, Daddy, and you used me to plan company get-togethers. I am worth more. I can *do* more." She glanced at Lawrence smirking on the other side of the table. "As for my so-called ridiculous decision to break off the engagement, I believe that is none of your business."

"You are my daughter, Cecily Camille, so it is my business."

"No, it's not. It's my life and my decision. I am doing what is best for me—."

"Maybe it's time to realize you need to do what's best for the Devereaux family name and my company."

Cecily closed her eyes and rubbed her forehead. A headache throbbed in the center of her head.

"Cecily? Are you okay?"

Lincoln stood behind her father, frowning. She hadn't noticed him come in.

"Lincoln! Thank God!" she blurted. She jumped to her feet and threw herself at him. She kissed his cheek.

He squeezed her waist. "Sorry I'm late."

"My hero," she whispered in his ear. "I'm so glad you're here."

Her father swung around, snorted loudly, and rose to his feet. "Dunn? What the hell are you doing here? Cecily, is this a joke?"

"Wh-what?"

"You didn't tell me your friend was Lincoln Dunn."

"You know Lincoln?" Cecily asked.

"Of course I do," her father said. "He works for Devereaux Industries."

Lincoln shook his head and grimaced. "Not anymore, Claude." He extended his hand, and Claude gripped it. "It's good to see you again, sir."

Cecily couldn't move. She stood frozen in place, staring at Claude and Lincoln.

He works for Devereaux Industries.

Lincoln nudged her, took her arm, and guided Cecily back into the booth. He reached for her hand, but she tucked the hand closest to him under her leg and picked up her drink with the other. Her head spun, and her appetite was gone. She downed her drink in two swallows and signaled their server for another.

Lincoln works for Devereaux Industries.

Her father narrowed his eyes and pursed his lips when their server set the second drink in front of her. She stared at him as she picked it up and took a sip.

Lawrence cleared his throat; Cecily had forgotten he was there. Her ex put his shoulders back and his chin jutted out, as he reached across the table to shake Lincoln's hand.

"I'm Lawrence, Cecily's fiancé." he said.

Cecily groaned and shook her head. "Ex-fiancé, Lawrence. You're my *ex-fiancé*."

Lawrence shrugged. "My apologies. There seems to be some confusion regarding our relationship status."

"No confusion," Cecily muttered. "We aren't engaged anymore. End of discussion."

Lawrence huffed. "Problem, CeCe?"

"Don't call me that," she snapped.

"Cecily, don't be rude," her father interjected. "It's unnecessary."

She pushed a hand through her hair and sighed. Lincoln slipped his arm around her shoulder and pressed a kiss to her temple.

"I don't think she was rude," he said. "She doesn't like being called CeCe. My guess is she was only reminding Lawrence not to call her by an unwanted nickname." Lincoln stared at Lawrence.

Her ex squirmed in his seat and scrubbed a hand over his face. He looked like he'd eaten a lemon as he mumbled, "Sorry."

Lincoln intimidated Lawrence, and Cecily loved it. Discovering her father's working relationship with Lincoln irritated her, but she pushed it aside. She focused on making her fake relationship with Lincoln seem real. Right now, she needed to convince her father and Lawrence that she was head over heels for Lincoln Dunn.

Cecily leaned into him, pressing herself tight against his side. She put her hand on his leg and squeezed, grinning at Lawrence and her father.

"What do you say we order dinner?" Cecily said.

Chapter 12

Lincoln

Lincoln glanced over at Cecily. She plastered herself against the passenger door, leaving two feet of distance between them and stared out the window, refusing to look at him. Cecily could have caught a ride with her father and Lawrence, but she went with Lincoln. It was obvious she didn't want to be in a car with her father or ex-fiancé, but Lincoln wasn't sure she wanted to be in the car with him either.

He couldn't blame her for wanting to avoid Claude and Lawrence; her father was overbearing, and Lawrence was an ass. Lawrence was also the fakest person Lincoln ever met, and he'd worked with politicians, musicians, and actors. The fake, deep voice he'd used most of the night—unless he forgot—made Lincoln repeatedly chuckle. The man had babbled incessantly about every topic under the sun, not allowing anyone else to speak. Lincoln could have dealt with those minor annoyances, but Lawrence's obvious disdain for Cecily was enough to make Lincoln want to take the guy out. And he wanted to make it hurt.

While dinner had been awkward and downright annoying, the car ride home felt like being suffocated with a wet blanket.

Lincoln cleared his throat. "Cecily?"

She refused to look at him; instead, she continued staring out the window with her chin propped on her hand.

"Will you talk to me, please?"

Cecily turned to look at him, and her voice broke when she spoke. "Why didn't you tell me you work for my father?"

He held the steering wheel with one hand and with the other hand, he rubbed the back of his neck. There it was; he'd waited all night for her to say something. He exhaled.

All right. Here we go. Honesty is the best policy.

"First, it's *worked*, not work. I am not currently employed by Devereaux Industries."

"Thanks for clarifying." Cecily's voice dripped with sarcasm.

Lincoln sighed and continued. "When we met, I didn't know you were Claude Devereaux's daughter."

"You didn't know? You worked for my father, and you didn't know I was his daughter? That seems unlikely."

"No, I swear." He chuckled nervously. "You told me your father kept you out of the spotlight. I gather he kept you out of his business dealings as well, or I would have seen you in a board meeting or something." He gripped the steering wheel so hard, his knuckles ached. "When I met you in New York, you were a gorgeous woman I wanted to spend the night with. And when I saw you at Time Out, you were the same gorgeous woman I still wanted to spend the night with. That's who you are to me, Cecily, a beautiful woman I am insanely attracted to. I didn't even know your last name. Believe me, I didn't know Claude Devereaux was your father until you mentioned it the other day. And I don't care who your father is."

Cecily snorted. "I've heard that before, Lincoln. You aren't the first man to feign a lack of knowledge about my father and my inheritance. I don't have the patience to deal with that again."

"What do you mean, again?"

Cecily pinched the bridge of her nose and stared at the lights flashing by the car window. "Every man I have ever dated is only interested in one thing—my father's money. It's difficult being the daughter of a billionaire. The last straw was Lawrence. I thought he loved me, but he was another guy using me to get to my father. Breaking off the engagement and moving to Montana hasn't staunched the love between my father and my ex-fiancé. It's a never-ending battle to prove to my father that Lawrence isn't who Daddy thinks he is; it's a battle I'm tired of fighting. I'm sick of it."

"I imagine you are. It can't be easy."

"No, Lincoln. It sucks. And now, apparently, I need to do it again."

"What?"

Cecily snorted. "You worked for my father. You're a successful businessman too. My father loves that, because it means a big, strong, smarter-than-her man could take care of his little girl. This whole fake relationship thing was a bad idea. I never would have asked you if I knew you worked for my father."

Lincoln grimaced. "I can assure you your father does *not* like me."

"He doesn't?"

"No, he doesn't. Trust me." He wasn't about to go into detail; Cecily had more than enough issues with her father. He didn't need to tell her the real reason he no longer worked for Claude Devereaux.

Cecily rolled her eyes, but a hint of a smile teased the corners of her mouth. "Okay, this is going to sound awful, but my father not liking you is good for our fake relationship. It takes the focus off Lawrence and me."

"And puts it on me."

She inched closer to Lincoln. "What? Do you think you can't handle it?"

Lincoln chuckled. "Oh, I can handle it. Your father doesn't scare me."

"Thank God, because sometimes he scares me." Cecily took Lincoln's hand and traced her fingers over his knuckles. "Did you really not know I was Claude Devereaux's daughter when we met?"

"I didn't, I swear. When we met, I didn't know who your father was. I like you for *you*, Cecily, not because you have money. I don't need *or* want your money."

Cecily laughed. "I've heard that before too."

"I'm sure you have. But this time it's true."

"What did you do for my father, anyway?"

He could tell her that much. "Cybersecurity consultants. After Van's wife died and he moved to Lakeside, we stepped away from personal security and started working in cybersecurity. There was a need, and we took advantage of it. It was easier with Van here and me in New York.

Devereaux Industries hired us to clean up their computer systems and increase their online security."

"How long did you work for him?" Cecily asked.

"Six months. Once we had the system up to par, we handed it off to his tech services and in-house security. We were back-up only, you know, in case of emergencies; that was three months ago."

Cecily took her hand out of his. "Wait a minute, we met three months ago."

Lincoln nodded. "Yes, we did. We met an hour after I left the board meeting." An hour after, he gave her father the finger and quit. He glanced at her out of the corner of his eye. The defeated look on her face broke his heart. Before he could react, she pointed out the window.

"Turn right at the stop sign."

Lincoln followed her directions, coming to a stop in a parking lot next to a long dock with several boats moored next to it. He put the truck in park, reached across the seat, and took Cecily's hand.

"I'm sorry someone with an ulterior motive has hurt you. But that's not me. This isn't some grand scheme to fool you out of your fortune or get in good with your father. Trust me, that is the *last* thing I want to do. When I say I don't want or need your money, I'm not lying. I do not need your money. Van and I recently sold our business for an enormous sum of money, enough that neither of us will ever have to work again."

Cecily tilted her head to one side and raised her eyebrows. "Really?" she whispered.

"Yes," he replied. "We sold the business two weeks after I met you. We were negotiating the sale while we still worked for your father."

"Okay, so you're not after my father's money. How come you didn't say something once you knew who I was?"

Lincoln shrugged. "I'm a chickenshit?" At least that earned him a genuine laugh. "Honestly? Every time I tried to tell you, something would happen—like best man speeches and servers playing with your dog. After two or three times of not saying anything, I figured it was too late. I was afraid you would hate me for not telling you, and you wouldn't want to spend time with me anymore. For that, I apologize; it was stupid and selfish."

Cecily squeezed his hand. "You are telling me the truth, right, Lincoln? I need to know because I can't handle any more deception, from anybody. I've been used too many times."

"I'm telling you the truth, I swear." He kissed the back of her hand and said, "I do not want or need your money. Now, are we okay?"

She sighed. "I guess so. But I need you to promise you won't withhold the truth from me again. Okay?"

"Yes, ma'am." He looped his pinky with hers. "Pinky swear." His gut clenched at the white lie slipping past his lips. Cecily didn't need to know her father was an ass and not quite legitimate with some of his business dealings. He would keep that from her, for the time being.

Cecily giggled, pulling his attention back to her. "You're a charmer, Lincoln Dunn. A real charmer."

"That's what I've been told." He wrapped his hand around the back of her neck, dragged her close, and kissed her. When he released her, he rested his forehead against hers and breathed her in, the intoxicating scent of orange blossoms filling his head. After a few seconds, he lifted his head and looked around.

"Where are we?" he asked.

Cecily smirked. "Um, the boat dock."

Lincoln rolled his eyes. "Obviously. I thought I was taking you home?"

She shook her head. "The boat is taking me home." She pointed at a sleek black-and-gold speedboat. "I live on the lake."

"Like, literally on the lake?"

Cecily laughed and waved her hand at the lake. "I live on an island, Devereaux Island. It's about three miles offshore."

He chuckled. "You never cease to amaze me."

Cecily kissed Lincoln's cheek, grabbed his hand, and clasped it between hers. "Thank you for the ride, and the explanation. I feel a lot better. Will you come to the house for brunch tomorrow? Please?"

Lincoln took her chin between two fingers, tipped her head back, and gave her a soft, lingering kiss. "Yes. What time?"

"I'll meet you here at ten." She pressed another kiss to his lips before she shoved open the truck door and jumped out. She jogged up the dock and climbed aboard the boat.

He sat and watched her get the boat ready until her father and Lawrence pulled into the parking lot and parked beside him. He tapped the horn twice, waved at Cecily, and left.

———

"How's the vacation?" Van asked. "Are you lying low?"

"Kind of," Lincoln replied. He propped the phone between his ear and shoulder while he drove. He didn't want to get lost in Lakeside trying to find his way back to the condo from the dock where he'd dropped off Cecily. The town looked a lot different in the dark.

"What do you mean by kind of?"

"I've been spending time with Cecily."

"Oh?"

"You don't have to sound so happy about it."

Van laughed. "You hear one syllable, and you think I sound happy."

"Yeah. You do, maybe even gloating a little."

"So, does this mean your total ban on relationships and love is over?"

Lincoln chuckled. "Hell, no. Cecily likes relationships about as much as I do; it's a mutual attraction. She's sexy and amazing in bed."

"TMI, brother."

"Sorry," Lincoln said. But he wasn't, not really. He'd been wanting to brag about Cecily for days, not just her prowess in the sack, but her personality, her determination, everything. He liked a strong woman, and Cecily fit the bill. "She's great, Van. Really great."

"Hmm," Van hummed.

"I know you want to say something. Spit it out."

"I think you're falling for this woman, Linc. This isn't like you. Spending time with women is not something you do. Ever since Cat screwed you over, you're a love 'em-and-leave 'em kind of guy."

"Nothing has changed," Lincoln snapped. He turned into the parking spot next to the condo and shifted the phone to his other ear as he parked the truck. "I'm on vacation, and I'm spending time with an attractive woman. The sex is great, and the company is great. In two weeks, I'm going back to New York: no attachment, no relationship. End of story." He slammed the truck door, unlocked the side door of the condo, and went inside.

"Are you trying to convince me or yourself?"

"I don't need to convince anyone of anything. I'm not getting attached. Cat taught me a lesson I will never forget. Look, I gotta go. I'll talk to you later." He disconnected the call and tossed his phone on the kitchen counter. It drove him crazy that Van knew him so well, the perils of being best friends for twenty-five years.

I am not falling for Cecily. Not at all.

Chapter 13

Cecily

Lawrence squeezed her shoulder before he sat on the chaise lounge beside her the next day. He glanced at the cup of coffee in her hand and smiled.

"There's coffee?" he asked.

Cecily looked at him over the top of her sunglasses. "In the kitchen, in the coffeepot. Mugs are in the cupboard to the left of the sink."

He snorted, rose to his feet, and stomped across the yard back to the house. Cecily giggled under her breath. She checked her watch; thirty minutes until she could take the boat to get Lincoln. He made an excellent buffer. Plus, she was pretty sure Lawrence was afraid of him.

Sebastian growled, signaling Lawrence's return.

"What is that dog's problem?" Lawrence muttered.

"He hates you," Cecily said.

"Wow, okay. Blunt much?" He sat back down and cleared his throat. "How did you sleep?"

"Fine."

"I saw Mrs. Tuttle making brunch."

"Yes."

"Is every conversation we have going to be like pulling teeth?"

Cecily shook her head. "Probably."

"Jesus, Cecily, enough already. You're pissed at me, I get it. I screwed up. I'm sorry. You've made your point."

"What do you mean, 'I made my point'?"

"I get it. I acted like an ass. It won't happen again. Can we move on?"

Cecily pulled her sunglasses off and stared at Lawrence. "I have moved on."

Lawrence took her hand. "I meant move on together. We can put the past behind us where it belongs and plan our future together."

"We don't have a future together, Lawrence. How many times do I have to tell you that?"

"Your father thinks we have a future."

"I don't care what my father thinks. He isn't in charge of my love life. I choose who I want to be with, not Claude Devereaux." She put her sunglasses back on and stared at the lake. "And I have Lincoln, now. I don't need or want you."

Lawrence waved his hand like he was shooing away a fly. "Both your father and I think Lincoln is a passing fancy. He'll move on soon enough, and you'll be alone again."

"Do you hear yourself when you talk, Lawrence? The things you say to me—."

"I'm trying to be honest," her ex snapped. "One of us should be." He looked pointedly at her.

Cecily shoved herself to her feet, snatched her sweater off the back of her seat, and picked up Sebastian. "I'm taking the boat to shore; Lincoln's coming for brunch. I'll be back in less than an hour."

The slam of the gate behind her left a satisfying ring in her ears. She unmoored the boat, put Sebastian in his life jacket, and secured him with his leash to the seat beside her. Within minutes, the speedboat skipped across the water, the wind blowing her long, black hair away from her face.

Cecily loved the water, and she loved the lake. Several times a week, she would take the boat out on the water and forget about her problems for a while. The ice-cold sprays of water hitting her skin revitalized and energized her, while the wind ruffling her hair and clothes reminded her of the power of nature. Flathead Lake was beautiful, a beauty difficult to explain to anyone who hadn't experienced it in person. She would never understand how her father could resist the charms of the lake. She wanted to stay here forever.

It took less than fifteen minutes to reach the dock. Lincoln lounged against one of the roof supports: sunglasses on, arms crossed, and muscles bulging.

How can this man look so incredibly delicious without even trying?

She waved at him as she pulled the boat alongside the dock. Lincoln waved back and jogged down the length of the dock to meet her.

"Are you ready?" she asked.

He grinned. "As I'll ever be." He jumped off the dock onto the bow, wrapped a hand around the back of her neck, and dragged her close. He leaned over her, his lips brushing hers as he spoke. "You look utterly delectable."

He caught her lips in his and kissed her breathless before moving down her neck and sucking at her pulse point.

Cecily's head fell back, and a shiver raced through her at the feel of Lincoln's lips on her skin. For a moment, she considered skipping brunch and going back to Lincoln's place. Sex with Lincoln would be more fun than brunch with her father and Lawrence.

She wrapped her arms around his neck and hooked a leg around the back of his thigh. "God, you're sexy," she whispered. "I could do you right here."

"Tempting offer, babe, but don't we have some-place to be?"

Cecily grimaced. "Yes. Unfortunately." She released Lincoln and returned to her seat at the helm. She looked over her shoulder at him. "You can sit back there. Seb rides shotgun. Do you want a life jacket?"

Lincoln chuckled and shook his head. He sprawled across the bench seat in the center of the boat, his long legs stretched out in front of him and his arms thrown over the back of the seat. "I'm good."

Cecily eased away from the dock. Once she cleared the dock and moved past the boats cruising the shoreline, she let loose, pushing the speedboat to the max. They sped across the water, bouncing across the waves, as sprays of water soaked into their clothes. She glanced at Lincoln several times; he had his head thrown back, and a huge smile on his face.

Why does he have to be so perfect?

When the house came into view, her stomach twisted uncomfortably. Brunch with Claude Devereaux and Lawrence was not as appealing as spending the day on the lake with Lincoln. She would have loved to show him the small cove with its gorgeous stretch of beach hidden on the other side of the island. It was easy to picture the two of them swimming in the clear blue water and making love on the sandy beach. Anything was better than what was to come.

Once she safely moored the boat, she tucked Sebastian under her arm and gestured for Lincoln to follow her up the dock. He took her hand, intertwining his fingers with hers. It felt right, natural. She swallowed past the lump rising in her throat.

What the hell is he doing to me?

Lawrence greeted them at the gate, a mimosa in his hand. He was unsteady on his feet as he reached for Lincoln's hand, wincing when Lincoln squeezed too hard.

"Are you drunk?" Cecily asked. "How is that possible? I was gone less than an hour." She put Sebastian on the ground and latched the gate.

Lawrence's eyes widened, and he snorted. He gave her a disgusted look before he turned to Lincoln. "How wonderful you could join us, Lincoln. We didn't get much of a chance to talk last night."

"Nobody had much chance to talk, Larry," Lincoln responded. "You talked enough for all of us."

Lawrence's eyes narrowed, and he waved the hand holding the mimosa in a circle. "I was only making conversation. Anyway, I have so many questions about how you and Cecily met." He gave her another pointed look before he gestured to a table by the pool laden with food. "I hope you're hungry; Mrs. Tuttle made enough food to feed an army."

Lincoln grinned. "I'm starving. A vigorous ride always makes me hungry." He winked at Lawrence, threw his arm over Cecily's shoulder, and headed for the table next to the pool.

Cecily slapped her hand over her mouth to muffle the laughter attempting to escape. She grabbed Lincoln's hand and squeezed it as a silent thank-you.

When Claude saw them coming up the walkway, he rose to his feet and extended his hand. He greeted Lincoln with a tight smile and gestured for him to sit. Cecily gave her father an odd look, but she bit her tongue.

"Good to see you, Dunn," Claude said.

Lawrence snorted, dropped into the chair beside Claude, and finished his drink. He grabbed the pitcher on the table and poured himself another one.

Claude eyed Lawrence up and down, then he tapped him on the shoulder and ordered him to move, so Lincoln could take his seat. His tone left no room for argument, so Cecily's ex got up and stomped to the end of the table. He sat down, grabbed a plate, and piled it high with food, glaring at Cecily, Claude, and Lincoln as he shoveled food into his mouth.

"What brings you to Montana, Lincoln?" Claude asked.

"Cecily."

"My daughter?"

Lincoln took a seat at the table next to Claude, reached for the plate of fruit and cheese, and popped a grape into his mouth. "Yes, sir."

"May I ask how you two met?"

"We met in New York—."

"I met him at a bar down the street from the hotel," Cecily interjected. "We got to talking and hit it off."

Claude crossed his arms over his chest. "When was this?"

Cecily sighed. "Daddy."

Lincoln smiled at her and squeezed her hand. "It's okay; it was three months ago, sir. Right after your last board meeting, I believe."

"No shit? Is that true?" Lawrence asked. "That's crazy."

"Why yes, Larry, it *is* crazy," Lincoln said. "Crazy that I saw a gorgeous woman drinking alone at a bar and wanted to get to know her better. One thing led to another, and here I am."

"Do you often fly across the country to visit women you've only known for three months?" Claude asked.

Lincoln chuckled. "Well, no sir. Turns out, it's a small world. As luck would have it, my best friend lives here in Lakeside. It was easy to plan a trip when I knew I could see both Cecily and Van."

"So, you're not here just for Cecily," Lawrence said. "Your friend is here too."

Lincoln took Cecily's hand and kissed the back of it. "Oh, trust me, I'm here for Cecily."

Cecily grinned at Lawrence and settled back in her seat. She poured herself a drink, as she listened to her father and Lincoln talk. The topics ranged from business to soccer, her father's favorite sport. Lawrence interjected occasionally, but mostly they excluded him from the conversation.

Once the food was gone and the pitcher of mimosas empty, Cecily excused herself and headed for the kitchen. She needed a break from her father giving Lincoln the third degree and Lawrence pouting. It was a testosterone-fueled nightmare on the patio, and Cecily had had enough.

"Cecily, are you hiding?"

Cecily popped up from behind the open refriger-ator door, seeing her father standing in the doorway. She grabbed a bottle of water, pushed the door closed with her hip, and sat on the stool at the large island.

"I'm not hiding; I needed a break."

"A break from what?" Claude sat on a stool opposite her.

"Everything." She cleared her throat. "So, do you like Lincoln?"

Claude shrugged. "Are you asking for my approval?"

She made a face. "No."

"I didn't think so." He cleared his throat. "He's suitable husband material."

Cecily rolled her eyes. "That's not what I asked."

"He will make someone a good husband someday."

"Someone?"

Claude nodded. "Yes, someone. It will not be you, though."

She took a sip of water and forced it past the lump rising in her throat. "Why is that?"

"I've heard rumors he's a bit of a ladies' man. My guess is that you are nothing more than a brief fling. Once he is done with you, he will move on."

Cecily recoiled, as if he had slapped her. "Daddy..."

"I know it hurts to hear that, princess. But it's true. You're better off with someone reliable, like Lawrence."

"Are you *ever* going to let that go? I don't love Lawrence."

"Be reasonable, Cecily; it's not always about love. You're thirty years old. It's time for you to quit messing around, hanging out on this stupid island in the middle of nowhere doing nothing with your life. Maybe if I cut off your trust fund—."

"You know what? Cut me off." She got to her feet. "I do not care." She emphasized each word with a tap of her index finger to the countertop.

Claude scowled. "I'm serious."

"So am I."

She wanted to say more, wanted to tell her father exactly what she thought of him, but before she could, she heard Lincoln outside.

"Sebastian, come back here!"

Cecily spun on her heel, sprinted through the house, and out the patio door. The back gate was open; Lawrence was on the dock; Lincoln was halfway across the lawn; and for the love of God, Sebastian was down by the water and headed for the woods.

"Sebastian!" she screamed.

Her dog froze and turned to look at her. He dropped his head and trotted back up the hill, his tail between his legs. She forced herself to stroll down the hill, so as not to spook the Shih Tzu and send him running away. When she reached him, she scooped him up and squeezed him hard enough to make him yelp in protest.

"Bad dog," she mumbled, as she plastered him with kisses. "Bad, bad dog."

Lincoln appeared at her side and slipped his arm around her waist. "I'm sorry. I tried to catch him. He wouldn't come to me; I don't think he trusts me yet."

"How did he get out?"

Lincoln looked at Lawrence. "Larry left the gate open."

Cecily shook her head. "Why am I not surprised?"

Lawrence met them at the gate. "Whoops. Thought I closed that gate." He winked at Cecily and took a swallow from the glass in his hand.

Out of the corner of her eye, Cecily saw Lincoln shake his head. She glared at Lawrence. "When are you going home?" she asked.

"We're leaving Tuesday morning," her father interjected from the patio. "I have a meeting in San Francisco in the afternoon."

Cecily gave both Lawrence and her father dirty looks. "It's not soon enough."

Chapter 14

Lincoln

After he returned from Cecily's, Lincoln took Van's boat out on the lake. He went to the spot Van considered the best fishing spot on the lake and spent three hours fishing. By the time he got back to shore, the sun was going down. A breeze kicked up, bringing a slight chill to the air. Every time he visited Montana, he forgot how cold it could get, even in the middle of the summer.

Back at the condo, he cooked a frozen dinner in the microwave and threw on a sweatshirt. Lincoln grabbed a six-pack of beer, the barely edible food, and went out on the patio. It might be cold, but the phenomenal view of the lake was worth sitting outside in the chilly breeze.

He wasn't sure what or how it happened. Cecily wormed her way into his brain and took up permanent residence. When he wasn't with her, he wanted to be. He thought about her all the time. He woke up with her on his mind, fell asleep thinking about her, and dreamed about her during the night. Cecily Devereaux consumed his every thought.

It scared the hell out of him.

Lincoln couldn't deny that they were good together. She made him laugh, made him feel like a kid, and she was by far the most gorgeous woman he had ever been around. When he acted like an ass, she called him on it. Cecily understood him on an emotional level he'd never experienced with anyone, other than Van. The physical side of their relationship was indescribable. Everything he had ever wanted in a woman was embodied in Cecily.

Dammit.

He had to tell her. After his marriage to Cat went south, he went to a therapist. During that time, he promised he would always be honest with himself and with the people in his life. Hiding his feelings from Cecily would not do either of them any good. If he was falling for her—and he was—then he owed it to himself, and her, to be honest about it. He had to tell her.

Lincoln pushed himself to his feet, grumbling under his breath about women worming their way into his head.

And my heart.

He threw his half-eaten microwave dinner in the trash and poured himself a glass of bourbon. He downed it and poured another glass. Back outside, he made himself comfortable with the bourbon and his remaining beer while he watched the sun drop below the horizon.

—

The fog of an alcohol-induced sleep weighed down Lincoln's body, and his head pounded like a mallet hitting a gong. He scrubbed a hand over his face and struggled to sit up. The bottle of bourbon had been a mistake.

With a loud grunt, he shoved himself upright. He groaned and clutched his head. It was too early, or he was too hungover. Probably the latter. He pinched the bridge of his nose, then he rubbed the sleep from his eyes.

Lincoln snatched his phone off the bedside table and checked it, seeing it was almost one in the afternoon. He'd slept half the day away. He dropped the phone back on the bed and made his way to the bathroom.

After his third glass of bourbon, the night became a blur. He wasn't even sure how he got to bed.

Lincoln stripped off his clothes and turned on the shower. He stepped over the edge of the tub and yelped as the frigid Montana water hit his skin, jolting him into full consciousness. He grabbed the soap and scrubbed himself clean. A shiver raced through him, as he stepped from the shower and wrapped a towel around himself.

The cold water woke him up, but it didn't stop his head from pounding. He needed a cup of strong black coffee. He threw on a pair of sweats and a T-shirt, grabbed his cellphone, and made his way to the kitchen. Once he had the coffee brewing, he opened the sliding glass door and stepped outside.

Lincoln took a deep breath and raised his face to the sun. Getting drunk last night hadn't helped him figure out how to handle the situation with Cecily; all it had done was give him a massive hangover.

In eight days, he was supposed to fly back to New York. He had eight days to figure out what he was going to do about this woman who had unexpectedly taken over his life.

As if on cue, his cellphone rang. He yanked it out of his pocket.

Speak of the devil, and she appears.

"Hey, gorgeous, how's it going?"

Cecily's garbled words were barely coherent. All he got out of her was it had something to do with Lawrence, and she was terrified.

"Whoa, whoa, slow down. What happened?"

Cecily choked back a sob. "I-I need your help. Can you come to the house? Please? I can send Mr. Tuttle to meet you at the dock."

"I'll meet him there."

"Thank you, Lincoln. Thank you so much."

"Anything for you, baby." The words were out of his mouth before he could stop them. He took a deep breath and chose his next words carefully before he blurted out something just as telling and stupid.

"Stay calm, and I'll see you in a while."

Shit. Damn woman, getting under his skin.

He shoved his phone in his pocket and headed for the bedroom to change. Lincoln to the rescue.

"So much for my coffee," he muttered.

———

Mr. Tuttle was in the boat, waiting for him when he got to the dock. Lincoln moved to the seat beside the caretaker and leaned close to be heard over the roar of the engine and the boat hitting the waves.

"What happened?" he asked.

"Sebastian appears to have gotten out last night," Mr. Tuttle explained. "Miss Cecily didn't realize he was gone until this morning. Mr. Lawrence left the gate open while he was in the garden, and Sebastian darted out. Mr. Lawrence claims he didn't notice the little dog leave the safety of the backyard, but he is not in the house or anywhere within the gates we've installed. We've looked all over, but the missus and I can only do so much. Miss Cecily is in a panic."

Lincoln shook his head. "I can imagine."

"She's been looking for him all morning. Alone. Neither her father nor Lawrence have bothered to help her. Mrs. Tuttle and I have tried, but neither of us can go too deep into the woods." Mr. Tuttle glanced at Lincoln out of the corner of his eye. "She didn't want to bother you, but she felt she had no other choice. She's worried you'll be angry with her or, worse, think she's being ridiculous."

Lincoln sat up straight as the boat approached Devereaux Island. "She loves that little guy. I get it. Dogs have the power to heal a person."

Cecily stood at the end of the dock, shifting from foot to foot, gripping her left hand with her right, and rubbing her palm with her thumb. She offered him a pained smile as he stepped off the boat.

"Thank you for coming, Lincoln."

He grabbed her elbow and pulled her into a hug. She buried her face against his chest, and, within seconds, gasping sobs escaped her. He held her close, rested his chin on top of her head, and rubbed her back.

"Hey, it's okay. We'll find him."

Cecily shook her head. "He's been gone so long. I'm not sure we'll find him. I mean, what if he went into the water or got hurt in the woods? What if a wild animal got him? He must be hungry and thirsty."

Lincoln had nothing to say. Cecily could be right, but he would do everything he could to find the little dog before he gave up hope.

"Where do you want to start?"

Cecily shook her head. "I don't know. I looked everywhere, but it was sporadic. I was all over the place."

Lincoln released her. "Let's get started."

Taking charge was in his nature, so he divided the area around the house into quadrants and handed out assignments. Mr. and Mrs. Tuttle oversaw the area around the mansion and inside the fence in case Sebastian came back. He and Cecily would search outside the fenced area, along the water and into the woods. He brought everyone together and gave them their instructions, then they set to work.

Two hours later, no Sebastian. They had walked along the edge of the lake, searched all the way around the huge Devereaux mansion, and gone a hundred yards into the woods, but he was nowhere to be found.

It didn't go unnoticed that Lawrence and Claude Devereaux were nowhere to be seen while everyone else searched. Cecily said her father was "busy working," and Lawrence was nose deep in his laptop. According to Cecily, neither of them had time to help her look for Sebastian. She shrugged it off, but Lincoln knew it bothered her. Now and then, he noticed Lawrence watching from the window. He never saw Claude.

Lincoln stood at the end of the path leading into the woods, waiting for Cecily. She had gone inside to get them something cold to drink. The temperature had jumped, especially after the chill in the air last night had worn off. It was close to ninety degrees.

He took several steps into the woods, off the path, into the trees. He hoped to hear a branch break, or maybe a bark or a whine, something, anything, that would lead him to Sebastian. Unfortunately, there wasn't anything.

"This is useless," he mumbled. He turned to head back to the house, but a faint yip stopped him in his tracks. He froze and strained to hear. Maybe it had been his imagination.

Then he heard it again, the distinctive whine of a dog. He took off in the direction he heard it coming from, pushing through the trees and bushes, calling Sebastian's name.

"Seb? Sebastian?"

A louder bark came from deeper in the woods. Lincoln followed the sound. Another fifty yards, and he saw a flash of white. He pushed through the brambles, bushes, and tall grass until he got to the dog.

Sebastian laid on the ground next to a tree, hidden under a large bush. His tail thumped weakly against the ground when he saw Lincoln, and he whined faintly.

"Hey, buddy," Lincoln whispered. "Are you okay?" He brushed a hand over the dog's back, wincing when Sebastian yelped. His left leg was oddly bent and covered in burrs, with long strands of grass wrapped around it.

"Alright, let's get you out of here." He gently brushed leaves and dirt off the dog, then he worked to untangle him. Sebastian watched him with his big brown eyes, whimpering quietly.

Lincoln scooped up the dog and hurried back through the woods. Cecily saw him coming up the path as she came out the back door, and when she saw her dog, she dropped the tray she carried on the table and ran down the path to meet them.

"Oh, my God, is he okay?" She reached for him but pulled her hands back at the last second when she saw his leg.

"I don't know. His left leg looks funny. I'm sure he's dehydrated too. Do you have a vet in Lakeside?" Lincoln asked.

"Dr. Schaffer. I'll call her." She pulled her phone from her back pocket. "Let's get him in the boat. You hold him, and I'll drive. The vet's office is on the water. She has a dock where we can put the boat."

Lincoln followed Cecily to the dock. As he settled himself and Sebastian on the boat, he glanced back at the house. Lawrence stood at the window, watching them with his arms crossed and a smirk on his face. If he'd been closer, Lincoln would have punched the smarmy look off his face.

Later.

Chapter 15

Cecily

"Thanks, Freddie. I'll pick him up Tuesday morning." Cecily ended the phone call and set her phone on the table. She stared out the sliding glass door at the moon shining on the lake.

Sebastian had been at the vet for hours. Dr. Winifred "Freddie" Schaffer had shooed her out of the office an hour after Cecily brought him in, promising to call as soon as she assessed his injuries and started treatment.

Cecily and Lincoln went to Lincoln's condo to wait; she wanted to be close in case Freddie wanted her to return to the office. Cecily paced and stared out the window while Lincoln watched a baseball game on the TV.

"How's Sebastian?" Lincoln asked from the couch.

Cecily smiled at him. "Sebastian's doing okay. He's sleeping, ate something, drank some water, and the vet tech gave him some pain meds. Freddie thinks the leg is broken. She's waiting for the swelling to go down to take the X-rays. If it is broken, he'll be in a cast for about six weeks. I can pick him up on Monday." Cecily swallowed past the lump rising in her throat. "I can't thank you enough for helping me find him. Nobody understands what Seb means to me—."

"I do," Lincoln interrupted. He rose to his feet and took two steps closer. "I know how a dog, or any pet, makes a difference in a person's life. Van's dog, Soldier, saved my best friend's life, more than once. Until Serena came along, Soldier was Van's only reason for living."

"Serena said Soldier saved *her* life."

Lincoln nodded. "He did. That dog, he's a hero, in more ways than one. So, I get it. Seb is important to you, so it was important that I help you find him."

Cecily crossed the room and threw herself into Lincoln's arms. She needed to feel his body against hers, fill her head with his scent, and have his powerful arms wrapped around her. She wanted him.

He hugged her close. "Hey, are you okay?"

"Yes. Thanks to you." She buried her face against his chest and inhaled. She took a second to center herself before she looked up at him. "Can I stay here tonight? I don't want to go back to the island. I am in no mood to deal with my father or Lawrence. Not tonight."

"Yeah, of course you can." He kissed her forehead.

Lincoln took her hand and led her to the couch. He sat down and pulled Cecily down with him, setting her between his legs. She toed off her shoes, rested her head on his chest, and closed her eyes. Lincoln put his hands on her shoulders, his thumbs digging into the knots at the base of her neck.

Cecily sighed and let her head drop, her chin resting on her chest. "That feels amazing," she whispered.

Lincoln worked his fingers into the stiff muscles in her shoulders and neck. It hurt, but it felt amazing. Her body went limp, relaxing under Lincoln's adept touch.

"How is it you make everything better?" she whispered.

Lincoln chuckled. "Do I? I thought I was just being a good friend."

Cecily tipped her head back and looked into Lincoln's gorgeous blue eyes. "You *are* a good friend. A fantastic friend."

Lincoln's lips brushed against the back of her neck. "Get some rest, sweetheart."

Cecily closed her eyes and exhaled. She rested her hands on Lincoln's thick thighs and let her head fall back against his chest again. She concentrated on Lincoln's hands on her neck and shoulders, the feel of his chest rising and falling under her head, and his manly scent washing over her. Within minutes, she was asleep.

———

"I appreciate you coming back to the island with me," Cecily said. "You didn't have to."

Lincoln squeezed her knee. "After you told me about your discussion with your father last night, I wasn't about to let you come back alone. I can only imagine what he and Lawrence have been plotting. You need a buffer."

The conversation Lincoln referred to had been more of a lecture on her father's part. It miffed him that she wasn't returning to the island after what he called her "adventure with that damn dog." He spent a half an hour going on and on about her responsibilities, his irritation with her, and her lack of respect for him, his money, and her place in his world. It took all her self-control not to hang up on him.

Lincoln helped Cecily dock the boat, then he took her hand as they walked to the house. She was grateful for the gesture, especially when she saw her father and Lawrence seated on the patio. Claude's crossed arms and scowl frightened her. Lawrence looked gleeful. She sighed and squeezed Lincoln's hand.

"Here we go," she muttered.

"Cecily," her father said, as they stepped through the gate.

She forced a smile onto her face. "Hello, Daddy."

Claude Devereaux rose to his feet. "Thank you for seeing Cecily home, Lincoln. Mr. Tuttle will take you back to town. Cecily, Lawrence, and I have things to discuss."

"What exactly do we have to discuss?" Cecily asked.

"Cecily's future," Lawrence said. "Something that is not any of your business, Mr. Dunn."

Lincoln took a step toward her ex-fiancé, but Cecily put her hand on his arm, stopping him. "My future is not anyone's business but mine," she said. "Therefore, there is nothing for us to discuss. Lincoln and I are going to the other side of the island. I am going to show him the cove, and we're going to have a picnic lunch."

Claude shook his head. "I don't think that's a good idea. There are things we need to talk about. Today."

This time it was Lincoln who shook his head. "I think Cecily has made it clear how she feels about staying here to discuss her future with two people who don't care what she wants. Come on, Cecily." He led her past them into the house and slammed the door.

"Are you tired of hearing me say thank you yet?" she asked.

Lincoln pulled her into his arms. "You can show me how thankful you are when we get to that cove you mentioned." He kissed her hard on the mouth and released her. "How fast can we get out of here?"

Turns out, they could get back on the boat in under an hour. Cecily avoided her father and Lawrence as she got everything together for a picnic and swimming, sticking to her bedroom, the linen closet, and the kitchen. She breathed a sigh of relief once they were back on the water and heading toward the opposite side of Devereaux Island.

She'd been wanting to take Lincoln to the secluded cove for days; it was the most beautiful spot on the entire island. Twenty-foot-high cliffs surrounded the crystal blue cove and trees dotted the small beach.

They dropped anchor twenty yards offshore. Cecily shucked off her cover-up, spread a towel on the bow of the boat, and stretched out. Lincoln pulled two bottles of beer from the cooler, sat down beside her, and handed her one.

She drank half of it, burped loudly, and wiped her mouth with the back of her hand.

Lincoln chuckled. "Have I told you how great you are?"

She turned to look at him, leaning on her elbow. "No, but I'm willing to listen to you expound on my greatness."

Lincoln cupped her face and brushed his thumb over her cheek. "You are great. Absolutely amazing."

"Lincoln," she whispered.

He put his thumb on her lips, silencing her. "Let me get this out before I chicken out." He leaned over her, his nose brushing hers. Her breath caught in her throat, and heat raced through her veins.

"I'm falling for you, Cecily. I know that's not what we agreed to or what you want to hear, but it's happening." He dragged in a deep breath. "You've consumed my soul, sweetheart, and I will not fight it. You can have me, all of me. I'm yours if you want me." He lightly kissed her, his lips just brushing hers, but it might have been the best kiss she'd ever had.

Cecily closed her eyes and focused on breathing. *Lincoln was falling for her. When did that happen? And how come the thought of her and Lincoln together, maybe forever, didn't send her running into the lake?*

"Lincoln, I—."

He cut her off, his mouth on hers, kissing her breathless. His hand was on her hip, squeezing and releasing repeatedly. Despite the sun beating down on them, goosebumps broke out across the surface of her skin.

Lincoln broke off the kiss and rested his forehead against hers. "How secluded is this place, sweetheart?" he whispered.

Cecily shrugged. "Nobody comes here; the island is private. We've worked hard to keep it that way."

Lincoln pushed her to her back, his hand between her legs, caressing her through her swimsuit. He was impatient, his lips on the inside of her thighs and the scruff of his unshaven chin scratching at her sensitive skin, sending exciting tingles through every nerve ending. He twisted his fingers in her plain black swimsuit bottoms and pulled them down her legs. A lusty moan escaped her when his lips touched her pussy.

His breath was hot as he lapped at her aching sex, while his fingers teased at her entrance. Cecily squirmed, desperate for more contact, desperate to get closer to him.

Lincoln planted one knee beside her leg and held tight to her hips, his fingers digging in and holding her brutally tight. He pushed himself forward as he tasted her, his tongue sliding deep into her. He pulled her close, his head moving from side to side, as the scruff on his face burned and his nose hit her clit.

Jesus Christ.

Lincoln moaned, hums of satisfaction coming from him that vibrated through her core. He slipped two fingers in beside his tongue and caressed her inner walls as his fingers moved in a come-hither motion.

"Oh, fuck, Linc, right there." Cecily gasped as he hit *that* spot, the perfect spot. She wrapped her hands around his head, her nails scraped his scalp, and her thighs closed around him, holding him in place.

Lincoln growled low in the back of his throat and his head came up, his eyes locking on hers. "Yeah, baby, that's what I want to hear." He dove back in, devouring her like she was everything he wanted and everything he needed. Muffled moans of sheer arousal came from him, adding to the vibrations rocketing through her.

Her hands flailed and reached for something, anything, to hold on to as unbelievable sensations rolled through her. She ended up grabbing the towel beneath her and holding it in a death grip as Lincoln fucked her senseless with his sinful mouth, her body completely at his mercy.

Wave after wave of pleasure assaulted her as Lincoln pushed her to impossible heights, and the orgasm exploded through her, so intense and so strong that for a brief second, she blacked out.

Cecily came to her senses a few seconds later to find Lincoln hovering over her, his hips nestled between her legs, his hands in her hair, and his lips on her neck.

"Holy shit," she whispered. "That was incredible."

Lincoln laughed. "It was fucking hot. And thank you for inflating my already substantial ego." He pressed a kiss to the underside of her jaw and rocked his hips into hers, his arousal rubbing against her sensitive center.

"Lincoln, about what you said."

"Not now, sweetheart. Later. I said my piece, and we're done." He kissed her again and intertwined his fingers with hers. "Let's just enjoy the rest of the day with no pressure."

Cecily nodded, but she had no intention of letting it go. They would talk about it before he flew off into the sun and headed east.

Chapter 16

Lincoln

Lincoln stood on the dock, locked in an embrace with Cecily, while Claude Devereaux stared down at them from a top-floor window of the mansion and the late afternoon sun shown down on them. His skin crawled like a thousand bugs had landed on him. He knew from experience that Claude was not a man to be reckoned with; not that he gave two shits about Claude Devereaux or his feelings about Lincoln's relationship with Cecily. It was obvious Claude didn't have Cecily's best interests in mind, or he wouldn't push her to marry a man she didn't love.

He was reluctant to leave Cecily, but she insisted she would be fine; she planned to go straight to her room and sleep through to the next day. It sounded like a great idea, one he intended to replicant once he was back at the condo. Not that it would be easy to fall asleep, as professing his feelings for Cecily had done a number on his head. He had a lot to process.

Cecily broke off the kiss and took a step back. "I'll call you tomorrow after I pick up Sebastian. I think we need to talk."

Lincoln sighed and nodded. He kissed Cecily one last time and turned to the boat where Mr. Tuttle waited to return him to the mainland. He waved at Cecily as the boat pulled away from the dock.

"Miss Devereaux seems quite fond of you, Mr. Dunn," Tuttle said.

Lincoln grinned. "You think so?"

"Oh, yes. Seeing her with you differs a great deal from seeing her with Mr. Bronson."

"I'm quite fond of her too," Lincoln said.

Mr. Tuttle smiled. "That's good to hear. It's been a long time since Cecily had someone on her side. After her mother died, her father changed. And Cecily was alone. Even after Lawrence came into her life, she was alone. It's good to see her smiling again."

Mr. Tuttle said nothing else as he pulled the boat up to the dock and Lincoln stepped off. He gave the caretaker a wave and headed for his truck.

Lincoln checked his watch as he parked in front of Serena's condo. After everything that had happened the last forty-eight hours, he'd forgotten what day it was. Van and Serena would be back Tuesday, which was tomorrow, and he was supposed to be back in New York on Friday.

He needed to talk to Cecily. He needed to know how she felt or if she was even interested in anything more than a sexual relationship.

Tomorrow. We'll talk tomorrow and figure everything out.

———

The knock on the door came far earlier than he expected, just after eight. He hadn't even poured himself a cup of coffee. Lincoln yanked the door open, expecting to see Cecily with Sebastian in tow, but he came face to face with Claude Devereaux.

Startled, Lincoln stepped back. "Mr. Devereaux. What are you doing here?"

And how did you find me?

"I need to talk to you, Dunn. About Cecily."

Lincoln's guard went up. He drew in a deep breath and exhaled. "What about Cecily?"

Claude pushed past Lincoln into the kitchen. "I want you to break up with my daughter. This nonsense has gone on long enough. Let her down easy and walk away. Lose her phone number and forget she exists."

Lincoln closed the door and turned to look at Claude. He kept his fists clenched at his sides. "I'm sorry. Nonsense? What nonsense?"

"You and Cecily. She has messed around for far too long. It's time for her to get back to work and settle down. No more games, no more dating random men to piss me off."

"Is that why you think she's dating me?" Lincoln interjected. "To piss you off?"

Claude gave him a terse nod. "Why else would she choose to date an ex-military man with a floundering security business?"

Lincoln snorted. *If only he knew.*

"Despite what you might think, Mr. Devereaux, your daughter is *not* dating me to piss you off. In fact, she didn't know that I knew you until a couple of days ago. Our relationship has nothing to do with you, nothing at all."

Claude glared at Lincoln and shook his head. "How much do you want?"

"What?"

Claude sighed and pinched the bridge of his nose. "I'm talking about money, Dunn. How much will it take to get you to walk away from my daughter?"

Lincoln's blood boiled. "There isn't enough money in the world, Mr. Devereaux." He pulled open the door and gestured to Claude's car in the driveway. "I think it's time for you to go."

Claude didn't move. He crossed his arms over his chest and waged a silent battle of wills with Lincoln, brown eyes locked with blue. Neither of them broke contact for almost a full minute.

Claude was the first to look away. He cleared his throat before speaking. "I don't think you understand. Cecily will marry Lawrence; it is non-negotiable."

"This conversation is over, Mr. Devereaux. Thank you for stopping by."

Claude stalked past him, not looking back until he was standing beside the car. He rested his hands on the roof of the car, hit the top of it with a fist, and turned back to Lincoln.

"End it, Dunn. Today. Or else." He didn't expound on what the "or else" might be. Instead, he climbed into the car and drove away.

—

Lincoln paced the back deck, his cup of cold coffee gripped tight in his hand. Cecily had texted him an hour ago to let him know she would be there soon.

He didn't know what to do. He wanted to tell her what happened with her father, but he feared it would upset her and push her to cut herself off from her father, the only family she had left. Lincoln didn't want to break up a family.

Out of the corner of his eye, he saw Cecily coming up the patio steps with Sebastian in her arms. The little dog looked half asleep and quite grumpy. Lincoln dropped his coffee cup to the table and held out his arms.

"How is he doing?" he asked.

Cecily handed Sebastian to Lincoln. "Good. The cast will be on for six weeks, then it will be more X-rays and possibly surgery to strengthen the leg. Freddie is worried he'll re-break it. She said if she puts a metal plate over the break, it should keep it from breaking a second time."

Sebastian stared up at Lincoln with his big brown eyes. He huffed and rested his head on Lincoln's shoulder. Lincoln rubbed a hand down his back several times before putting him on one of the padded patio benches. With his broken leg jutting out awkwardly from his body, Sebastian laid down and closed his eyes.

Cecily wrapped her arms around Lincoln's waist, pushed up on her toes, and pressed a kiss to his cheek.

"Hi," she whispered.

Lincoln smiled down at her. "Hi, gorgeous. How was your night?"

She shrugged. "I hid in my room, like I said I would. Mrs. Tuttle even brought my dinner upstairs so I didn't have to endure another meal with my father and Lawrence. She told them I was sick. They left early this morning without even saying goodbye."

Lincoln rolled his eyes. "Your father left without saying goodbye??"

"Yes. Lawrence didn't come and bug me, and when I came downstairs this morning, they were gone. I had to wait for Mr. Tuttle to come back with the boat before I could get Seb."

He tightened his hold on Cecily, pulled her tight against his body, and kissed her, hard.

"What was that for?"

"I just wanted to kiss you." He cleared his throat. "I need to tell you something."

Cecily took a step back and pinched the bridge of her nose. "Is it going to be something I'm going to lose sleep over? Because the last thing you told me kept me awake all night."

"I'm sorry about that—."

Cecily waved her head, dismissing his apology. "Don't apologize. I'm grateful you were honest with me. I prefer that to hiding your true feelings from me. It just gave me a lot to process and think about." She sat on the patio bench beside Sebastian, rested her hand on his flank, and scratched him. "What did you need to tell me?"

"Your father stopped by on his way out of town."

Cecily's eyes widened, and her shoulders stiffened. "I'm sorry, what? My father stopped here? Why would he do that?"

Lincoln sighed. "He asked me to break up with you. He insisted your marriage to Lawrence was inevitable."

The look on her face broke his heart. She sighed and stared out over the lake as she spoke. "I do *not* understand him. He refuses to let go of this thing with Lawrence. He sabotages all my efforts to get a job, and he won't be happy until I'm back in New York, working for his stupid, precious company."

Lincoln sat down beside her and slipped his arm around her waist. He pressed a kiss to her temple. "Maybe it's because he worries about you? Maybe he thinks if you're in New York, he can monitor you and keep you safe."

Cecily snorted. "My father isn't that noble, Lincoln. It's a control thing for him. Plain and simple. If I'm in New York, he can keep me under his thumb and force me to do what he wants." She rested her head on Lincoln's shoulder. "He refuses to let me live my life. You know, he's threatened several times to cut me off if I won't abide by his rules. Maybe it's time I let him. I don't want his stupid money, anyway. It causes me nothing but grief."

"Is that what you want?" Lincoln asked.

She shrugged. "Maybe. I don't know. I'm not sure what I want. Speaking of which, let's talk about what you want."

"What?"

"I know you're trying to avoid talking to me—."

Lincoln shook his head. "No, I'm not, I swear."

Cecily smiled. "Okay, whatever you say. But we need to talk. You sprung some serious stuff on me yesterday."

Lincoln tried to interrupt her again, but Cecily put her finger on his mouth and shushed him.

"I'm not done." She took a deep breath. "I like you, Lincoln. A lot. Far more than I should like you. Whatever this is between us wasn't supposed to be anything more than a minor fling, a blip on my radar. You were supposed to be out of my life in two weeks. We were going to walk away, remember? Maybe as friends, maybe not. Instead, you swoop in and tell me you have feelings for me. You

tell me I've consumed your soul. How the hell am I supposed to respond to something like that?"

"Tell me how you feel," Lincoln whispered.

Cecily shook her head. "That's just it. I don't *know*
how I feel. I haven't allowed myself to think about it." She
pulled herself out of his arms, rose to her feet, and stared
at the lake. "I'm scared to think about."

He had to ask the obvious question. "Do you want a
relationship?"

Cecily shrugged. "If you asked me that question two
weeks ago, before you got here, the answer would have
been an adamant no. But now, I don't know."

Lincoln jumped to his feet and crossed the patio in
two long strides. "Take everything else out of the equation:
the money, your father, Lawrence. If none of that was clog-
ging up your brain, what would your answer be?"

Her shoulders slumped, and she shook her head. "I
can't process this without that stuff. It's impossible." She
scooped up Sebastian and turned back to Lincoln. "I
should go. The last twenty-four hours left me feeling... dis-
combobulated. I need to think. I'll call you later."

"Cecily."

She froze at the top of the patio steps, but she didn't
turn around. "Give me a little time, Lincoln. Let me figure
out what I want."

Instead of following her around the side of the house
or trying to convince her to stay, he let her go. She took
her little dog and left.

You can't force someone to love you.

If anybody knew that, it was Lincoln Dunn.

Chapter 17

Lincoln

"Lincoln!"

He swung around just in time to catch the enormous ball of fur flying at him, stumbling back several steps when the Belgian Malinois's full seventy pounds hit him. Lincoln hefted him into his arms and endured thirty seconds of having his face licked before he set Soldier on the ground.

"What are you feeding him? He weighs a ton."

Van laughed and reached out to hug his best friend. "Serena sneaks him table scraps when I'm not looking. She thinks I don't know, but I do."

"When did you get back?" Lincoln asked. "I didn't see you coming from your condo."

Van clapped him on the back. "An hour ago. I was on my way over when I saw you headed for your car. Where are you going?"

"I thought I'd go to Time Out for a burger and some beers. You should come with me."

"I'm here to ask you to come over and have pizza with us. Serena ordered one from Roselli's. And we've got beer."

"I don't want to intrude."

"You're not. I'd like to spend some time with my best friend before you head back to New York. You're leaving Friday, right? Besides, we are insanely curious to hear about you and Cecily."

"We? So, you told Serena?"

"Yeah, of course. No secrets between married couples, right?"

Lincoln raised an eyebrow and snorted.

Van grinned and shrugged. "Cat doesn't count; she never loved you like you deserved."

Lincoln flinched. "Thanks for the reminder."

"Come on. Quit being an ass and come have dinner with us. Right, Soldier?"

Soldier barked and wagged his tail.

"Fine. I'll come have dinner with you." Lincoln rolled his eyes. "Promise me no third degree, though, okay? I know you're curious about Cecily and me, but it's still new. Different. I'm not even sure where it's going or if it's even going anywhere."

"Take my dog for a walk and meet me back at my place." Van tossed Soldier's leash to Lincoln. "I'm going to go pick up the pizza."

—

"Start talking."

"Serena." Van made a slicing motion across his neck and tapped her leg with his foot.

"No, don't 'Serena' me. We've waited long enough. Lincoln got to hear all about our honeymoon. We ate pizza, and we drank beer. Now, he talks."

Lincoln laughed. "What exactly am I talking about?"

Serena gave him a dirty look, but a smile teased the corners of her mouth. "Cecily. I want to know everything."

"Everything?"

Serena giggled. "Maybe not everything. You can leave out anything about sex." She made a face.

Lincoln jumped to his feet. "Great. I'll see you two later."

"Sit down!" Van ordered. Soldier barked his agreement.

"I'm going to need another beer for this." He stepped into the small kitchen and pulled one out of the fridge. "Anyone else?"

Van raised his hand, but Serena declined. She sat back in her chair, crossed her arms over her chest, and waited.

Lincoln made them wait, staring out the window, stopping to pet Soldier, and drinking his beer. It wasn't until Serena cleared her throat that he talked.

"I like Cecily. A lot."

A grin spread across Serena's face. "You do?"

Lincoln nodded. "Yes, Serena, I do."

"I'm going to be a buzzkill and ask the obvious question," Van interjected. "I know your history, bro. All of it. So, I have to ask. Are you serious about this woman? Or are you going to go home to New York on Friday and forget she exists?

Lincoln scrubbed a hand over his face. "Always asking the hard questions. I like her, Van. I will not forget she exists."

"Do you think she might be *the one*?"

He shrugged. "I don't know. Do I want her to be the one? Yes, I do. Does she want to be the one? I don't know."

Serena's mouth fell open. "You don't know?"

Lincoln laughed. "No, Serena, I don't. Cecily wasn't—or isn't—any more interested in a relationship than I am. I really took her by surprise when I told her I have feelings for her. I think I scared her." He sat on the couch next to Van. "Then there's her father."

"Claude?" Van asked.

"Yep."

Van sat forward, his elbows on his knees and a scowl on his face. "What did Devereaux do?"

"He offered to pay me off if I broke up with his daughter."

Van shook his head. "Why am I not surprised?"

"What kind of person does that?" Serena said.

"Claude Devereaux," Lincoln replied. "He is *exactly* that kind of person. Manipulative and controlling. He will do anything to keep Cecily under his thumb, which includes making her marry Lawrence."

"Who's Lawrence?" Van asked.

"Her ex-fiancé," Serena explained. "They broke up six months ago and from what she's told me, her father won't let it go."

Lincoln nodded. "It's true. I cannot understand why. I had the pleasure of meeting Lawrence, and honestly, he's a jerk. He treats Cecily with aloof disdain, scoffs at her every word while also begging her to take him back. And her father sees how he treats her, witnesses it firsthand, but he wants them to get married. Devereaux doesn't give a shit what Cecily wants. It's crazy."

Serena let out a low whistle and shook her head. "I knew Cecily had issues with her father, but I did not know it was that bad."

"I'm assuming you told him to piss off," Van said.

Lincoln chuckled. "In not so many words. He wasn't impressed. But guess what? I don't give a shit."

Van laughed. "I figured as much." He leaned forward and put his elbows on his knees. "So, what are you going to do about Cecily?"

"I'm going to let her decide what she wants. I don't think she needs another man in her life telling her what to do." Lincoln checked his watch and pushed himself to his feet. "Look, it's after ten, and I have imposed on you long enough."

"You're not imposing." Serena said.

Lincoln squeezed Serena's shoulder and smiled down at her. "Yes, I am. You don't need me hanging around. You're still on your honeymoon."

Eyes downcast and a blush coloring her cheeks, Serena patted his hand and giggled. She jumped to her feet, grabbed her beer, and said, "Come on, Soldier. Let's get your leash and go for a walk."

Van caught her around the waist, pulled her close, and kissed her softly on the cheek. "I'll catch up with you."

Serena brushed a kiss across Van's lips, then she snapped her fingers, drawing Soldier to her side. She headed for the door, grabbed Soldier's leash off the table, and waved goodbye to Lincoln. Van watched Serena from the patio overlooking the lake until she disappeared into the shadows.

Lincoln envied him. Van's love for Serena and her love for him was the purest, sweetest, greatest love he'd ever seen. He didn't think he wanted love; shit, he didn't think he deserved love, but it snuck up on him and punched him in the gut. And damn it, he wanted it, and he wanted it with Cecily.

Van stepped back inside and returned to his seat. He leaned forward, his elbows on his knees. "It seems odd that her father is pushing for the marriage, despite Cecily's reservations."

"You mean despite her outright refusal? You're right. It is odd."

"Have you investigated Lawrence? Done a deep dive into his history?"

Lincoln shook his head. "It seemed invasive."

"Would you object to me running his name through the system?" Van asked.

"You think you might find something?"

Van shrugged. "Maybe, maybe not. But it can't hurt to look. Maybe he's got money issues, or he's power-hungry. Maybe he has some shit on Claude. Who knows? Let me check him out."

It took him two seconds to decide. "Do it."

Lincoln said his goodbyes and crossed the street to Serena's old condo. His eyes were heavy, and his head felt like he stuffed it with cotton. Sleep beckoned him. Hopefully, it didn't elude him.

Once he stripped off his clothes, he fell onto the bed and within seconds, he was asleep and dreaming of Cecily.

Chapter 18

Cecily

Cecily delivered Sebastian to the island, leaving him with Mrs. Tuttle to fuss over his injuries. She returned to the boat and headed for open water, pushing the throttle open until the boat flew across the crystal blue lake. The wind tied her long black hair in knots, and water drenched her clothing. She didn't stop until there was no land or other boats to be seen.

It was a gorgeous day, one of those rare Montana days where the temperature hovered around ninety degrees and there wasn't a cloud in the sky. Cecily cut the engine, dropped the anchor, pushed her hair out of her face, and climbed onto the bow of the boat. She stretched out and stared at the endless blue above her.

This was her safe space; it had been for years. She came out here when the thoughts in her head became too much to sort out. It had been a crazy ten days. Everything jumbled together, making it hard to focus on one thing:

Lawrence; Lincoln; her father; the never-ending arguments about her canceled engagement; sex with Lincoln and unwanted feelings developing. Even Sebastian fought for space in her head.

Cecily sat up, raised her head to the sky, and screamed as loud as she could. She didn't stop until her throat was raw and the sound faded to almost nothing. She flopped back on the bow, spreadeagle. Her heart pounded, and her breath tore in and out of her throat.

Lincoln wasn't supposed to fall in love with her. This was supposed to be a fling; two weeks, in and out, and then they moved on. Instead, Lincoln threw a monkey wrench in the system and announced he had feelings for her.

Feeling's mutual, buddy.

There it was, the thing she avoided facing for the last eighteen hours.

I'm in love with Lincoln Dunn.

Cecily closed her eyes and turned her face toward the sun. "I'm in love with Lincoln Dunn," she said out loud. She wanted to hear the words, feel them wash over her as she admitted to herself that she was indeed head over heels for Lincoln.

"Dammit," she muttered. "How did that happen?"

There was no question how it happened. Lincoln was sweet, protective, handsome, and an unbelievable lover. He saved her dog, and he helped her out when he didn't have to. The real question was why had it taken her so long to realize she loved him?

The next question was, now what? Should she run to Lincoln like a woman in some cheesy movie, jump into his arms, and the two of them could live happily ever after? Was it even possible?

This was unfamiliar territory for her. Lawrence had pursued her, not giving up until she agreed to go out with him. Her love for Lawrence grew while they dated, but it never became a deep, gnawing need in the pit of her stomach. Not like Lincoln. He owned her mind, her body, and her soul. Lincoln possessed her.

She sighed, and her worries seemed to float away like a child's balloon stolen by the wind. A calmness settled over her, and her worries disappeared. Figuring out what she wanted was half the battle. She wanted Lincoln Dunn; the rest would work itself out.

The gentle rocking of the boat and the warm sun lulled her to sleep.

—

Cecily woke when cold water droplets hit her bare skin. She shot up, worried the boat broke anchor, and had drifted close to shore, but it was a late afternoon rain sprinkling the watercraft. Typical Montana weather; gorgeous in the morning, rain in the evening. She scrambled off the bow and into the driver's seat.

It took thirty minutes to get back to Devereaux Island. Fortunately, the rain wasn't heavy, and it was still light out, though the chill in the air made her shiver. Her stomach growled, and her throat was dry. After lying in the sun for hours, she probably had a sunburn too.

Cecily docked the boat and checked her phone as she made her way to the house. There were no calls, no texts, and no voicemails. It was unfathomable to her that neither her father nor Lawrence had contacted her since they left. But rather than relief, a sense of foreboding had settled over her. She didn't trust her father or Lawrence, and her fight with them was far from over.

It's just the beginning.

"Mrs. Tuttle?" she called, as she pushed open the enormous oak door and stepped into the foyer. She threw her bag on the table by the door. "Mrs. Tuttle?"

The only answer was a faint bark. Cecily followed the sound until she found Sebastian contained in the small room under the stairs she had converted into the dog's bedroom. She equipped it with a large, soft bed, food, and water dishes, and a basket full of toys. Taped to the bottom of the Dutch door was a note.

Ms. Devereaux-

Mr. Tuttle and I have gone to town for dinner.

Sebastian will need to be fed. He was very mopey this afternoon and wouldn't eat.

Also, your father left a note for you on his desk. You should read it.

Have a wonderful evening!

Mrs. Tuttle

Sebastian hobbled to the door and stared up at her. She opened the Dutch door, scooped him up, and planted a kiss on the top of his head. In the kitchen, she prepared his food while he watched her. Once he had his food, she went down the hall to her father's office, pushed open the door, and stepped inside.

Propped in the center of her father's desk was a letter, her name written across the front in his neat, almost-perfect handwriting. She sat in the enormous leather chair behind the mahogany desk and stared at the letter for a full minute before she picked it up, holding it between two fingers as if it might bite her.

Cecily took a deep breath, opened the envelope, removed the letter, and unfolded it.

Cecily-

I know you are angry and frustrated. I understand your independent streak, perhaps better than you. But I've indulged the fun and games long enough. It's time to give up the childish wares and take on your adult responsibilities. Lawrence is suitable marriage material, far better than Lincoln Dunn, a going-nowhere former military man with a reputation as a ladies' man. An alliance with Lawrence will be an asset to you and, ultimately, to Devereaux Industries. I expect you to return to New York by the end of the month or forfeit your trust fund. No further discussion is necessary.

Sincerely,
Claude

She wanted to scream. *An alliance with Lawrence? What did that mean?* Her father worded it like she was some damsel being sold to a suitor to benefit her father's kingdom.

Cecily sat up straight, the letter falling from her fingers and fluttering to the ground.

"Son of a bitch!"

—

Four hours and a pounding headache later, Cecily sat at the dining room table, leafing through page after page of internal Devereaux Industries communications, as well as her father's private notes. Her father's use of the word "alliance" had seemed odd, odd enough that it prompted her to suspect something nefarious might be happening at the company.

It took her an hour to get into the private accounts and notes on the Devereaux servers. Thankfully, her father was a creature of habit and had never changed his password from "deirdreandclaude"; it had been the same thing for years. She memorized it in grade school to access the home internet. It hadn't taken much detective work to find her father's private files. From there, she searched her name, and then Lawrence's name, and discovered a wealth of information.

Lawrence Bronson was the son of Gerald Orville Fortuna. The Fortuna crime family was well known up and down the East Coast. They had ties to drugs, prostitution, and illegal gambling. Her father had done business with them for years, using Devereaux Industries' various companies to launder their illegal money. Gerald Fortuna paid her father insane amounts of untraceable cash in return.

According to the emails Cecily uncovered, Claude had second thoughts about his business dealings with Fortuna. He wanted to break free, but Fortuna refused to let him out of the business. The tone of the emails changed from mildly worrisome to downright threatening. Claude backed down and apologized for suggesting they part ways.

Unconvinced, Gerald Fortuna threatened to ruin Claude's business and his reputation. He demanded a promise from Claude, a deal to keep their business dealings intact in perpetuity. Gerald's suggestion—a marriage between their children.

Cecily dropped the papers to the table and pushed herself away from the table. She stumbled into the kitchen, leaned over the sink, and vomited. She rinsed out the sink, sank to the floor, and put her head on her knees.

Her father traded her to keep his business and reputation from falling to ruin. She was nothing more to her father than an object meant to be used as he saw fit. Her marriage to Lawrence was an alliance between a prominent crime family and a powerful entrepreneur. Love had nothing to do with it.

Bile rose in her throat again, but she forced it back down. She'd had enough information for one night, so she dragged herself to her feet and pulled open the cabinet next to the sink. She grabbed four ibuprofen and a sleeping pill, filled a cup with water, and swallowed them. Sebastian was asleep under the table, so she picked him up and carried him to her room.

It wasn't until she was in bed, buried under the blankets, that her mind turned to Lincoln. The recent revelations about her life had her second-guessing everything. *Did she really love Lincoln?* After what she'd just discovered, she wasn't sure she knew what love was. They had fooled her once. She wouldn't be fooled again. Maybe loving someone or even someone loving her wasn't meant to be. For all she knew, it was all another lie.

Chapter 19

Cecily

The phone rang six times before Cecily gave up.

His phone must be on silent.

It was early, just after seven, and she had only been awake for about five minutes. She hadn't been able to wait another minute to talk to Lincoln.

Not only did she need to talk to him about their relationship and where it was going, but she needed his advice. He knew her father, he'd worked for her father, and he'd implied that he didn't care for her father's business practices. She convinced herself talking to Lincoln would make her feel better. Maybe he could ease her mind and tell her she was wrong, that her engagement to Lawrence wasn't a penance her father had to pay to crime boss Gerald Fortuna. Better yet, maybe he had proof she imagined the whole thing.

Just the thought of being used as a pawn in a business deal drove the nausea from the previous night back to the surface. She scrambled out of bed and rushed to the bathroom, her head hanging over the toilet for several minutes, though her empty stomach kept her from vomiting.

She scooped up Sebastian and headed for the kitchen, where she grabbed a bottle of ginger ale. Her stomach settled after a few sips. She distracted herself by getting Sebastian's food ready for the morning and making a pot of coffee.

Maybe I should call my father.

Even contemplating talking to her father made her nauseous all over again. *What was she supposed to say? "Hey Dad, I found out you were trying to use me as a bargaining chip in your dealings with a known mobster." Cringeworthy.*

A faint bark drew her attention to the back door. Sebastian stared at her, then he scratched at the door, a forlorn look on his cute, little face. He wanted out, and she was ignoring him. Cecily opened the door and followed him out. He limped across the yard, the leg in the bulky blue cast stuck oddly out behind him. He spent a few minutes sniffing around the patio table, did his business under the bush, and laid down under one of the chaise lounges.

Cecily checked the gate to make sure she latched it before she went inside for coffee. She took a mug out of the cupboard and some cream from the fridge.

"Good morning, Ms. Devereaux."

Cecily jumped and swung around, a high-pitched squeak leaving her.

"Mrs. Tuttle! You scared me to death!"

Mrs. Tuttle laughed. "My apologies. How was your day yesterday?"

Cecily grimaced. "It kind of sucked."

Mrs. Tuttle made an odd face. "I'm sorry to hear that. Anything I can do?"

"I don't think so," she replied. "By the way, thank you for watching Sebastian."

"It was my pleasure. You know I love that little dog almost as much as I love you."

Cecily set her mug on the counter, bounded across the room, and pulled Mrs. Tuttle into a tight hug. Mrs. Tuttle gasped.

"I love you too," Cecily mumbled. She kissed the woman's cheek, then released her.

Mrs. Tuttle patted her hair, as if her tightly woven braid would dare release a stray hair. She cleared her throat. "I think I heard your cellphone ringing. Did you leave it upstairs?"

Cecily rolled her eyes. "Yes, I did. Thanks. I'll go grab it."

Her phone was on the bathroom counter. She checked her missed calls. The only one she had was from Lincoln. She hit the button to call him back.

"Hey, sweetheart," he answered.

"Thank God, Lincoln. I need to talk to you."

"I gathered as much since you called me at seven in the morning. Are you okay?"

"Yes." She dragged in a deep breath. "No, that's not true. I'm not okay. In fact, I am so not okay I want to scream. I need to talk to you, and I don't want to discuss it on the phone. Can you meet me? Please?"

Lincoln warily agreed. She couldn't blame him; he'd bent over backwards for her during the last week, helping her with her father and ex-fiancé, her dog, and now she needed him again. He probably thought they were going to talk about his feelings for her and if she reciprocated them. Instead, she needed yet another favor from him. Maybe she should clarify what she needed from him.

"Cecily?"

She snapped back to reality. "Sorry. My mind drifted. Meet me at The Farmhouse on Stoner Loop. Do you need directions?"

"I'll find it. What time?"

"In an hour?" she asked.

"See you then." Lincoln disconnected the call.

Cecily sighed as she shoved her phone back in her pocket. She didn't like Lincoln's short, clipped sentences and irritated tone.

I might have pushed my only ally too far.

If he walked away from her at the end of his two-week vacation and never talked to her again, she wouldn't blame him one bit.

—

Lincoln pushed open the door, looked around the small restaurant, and headed for the table Cecily grabbed at the back of the restaurant. He slid into the booth across from her and folded his hands in front of himself, squeezing them so tight she heard his knuckles crack.

"Hi."

After tipping his chin in her direction, he signaled their server and ordered a coffee. He picked up the tiny cup and downed the black coffee in three swallows. He winced and set the cup back down.

"Sorry. I didn't sleep well. I need a heavy dose of caffeine." He gestured to their server and pointed at his coffee cup.

"I understand; I didn't sleep well, either."

Their server took their breakfast order and refilled their coffee. Lincoln waited until the young man walked away before he spoke. "All right, I'm here and slightly caffeinated. What's up?"

Cecily cleared her throat. "I have a question for you." She shifted in her seat, sitting up as straight as possible, her back resting against the cold vinyl of the booth and her toes just brushing the floor. "How much do you know about my father's business?"

Lincoln sighed. "Quite a bit. Why?"

He was being intentionally evasive. "I want you to tell me why you quit. Tell me why you dislike my father so much. Most people love him, think he's charming and wonderful. Not you."

His eyes narrowed and his shoulders stiffened. "Cecily, I can't discuss my business dealings with your father. Devereaux Industries required an NDA when Van and I went to work for them. I will say that my ideas about proper business practices did not mesh well with your father's. Aside from that, I cannot share anything with anyone, including you."

Cecily huffed and crossed her arms. "This is my father's company. I have a right to know what he is doing."

"Then ask your father. I can't tell you."

"Lincoln, come on."

He scrubbed a hand over his face. "I'm serious, sweetheart. I can't tell you anything, not unless I want to cost Van and myself a crap ton of money."

"My father is in deep with Gerald Fortuna. You know who that is, right?"

It was Lincoln's turn to clear his throat. "Yes, I do. I can tell you that Fortuna is not a man to be trifled with. If your father pissed him off…"

"Lawrence is Fortuna's son."

Lincoln jerked in his seat, his knee hit the table, and his coffee sloshed over the side of the cup, staining his napkin. "How did you find out?"

"Wait? You knew?"

"I know *now*," Lincoln said. "I didn't know before this morning." He cleared his throat. "Van offered to investigate Lawrence. I told him to do it. I called him on my way over here, and he filled me in. Lawrence used his mother's maiden name to avoid complications with the law."

Cecily sighed. "I didn't know he was Fortuna's son. I had no idea. Fortuna and my father were behind the engagement, a deal to guarantee their business arrangement lasted forever. I found paperwork, emails, a bunch of stuff that made it clear my father used me to keep Fortuna happy. But since I broke it off, I messed everything up. No wonder my father is desperate for us to get back together."

"You think your father arranged your marriage to Lawrence? As what, a payment to Gerald Fortuna?"

"Yes. Sick, huh?"

Lincoln pushed himself out of the booth and slid in next to her. He put his arm around her and squeezed. "Jesus, Cecily, I don't know what to say. 'I'm sorry' doesn't seem like enough."

She rested her head on his shoulder and closed her eyes. "I don't want it to be true. What kind of person uses his child as leverage in a sick business deal?"

Lincoln grunted. "What are you going to do?"

"I don't know. The thought of talking to my father terrifies me."

"I could talk to him. I'm going back to New York tomorrow—."

Cecily cut him off. "Thank you, but this is something I need to take care of myself. If I don't stand up to Claude, I'll always be afraid of him. My father treats me like I'm a helpless, clueless female. I need to prove to him I'm not. I'm going to stand up for myself. He will be told who is in charge of my life." She squeezed his arm. "So, you're leaving tomorrow?"

"I couldn't get a flight out of Kalispell, so I'm going to Missoula tonight. My flight leaves early tomorrow morning." He propped his arm on the back of the booth and turned to face her. "I guess that means our two-week one-night stand is over."

Cecily twittered nervously. "Cute."

"Cute? Okay, if you say so." He chuckled. "So, tell me, did you think about us?"

"I did." She picked at the napkin on the table, shredding it to pieces. Her stomach rolled and her head spun. This wouldn't go well.

He twisted a strand of her hair around his fingers. "I wonder, what conclusions did you reach?"

"My life is upside down, Lincoln. I don't know whether I'm coming or going. I don't even know if I can trust you."

Lincoln closed his eyes and snorted. "You *know* you can trust me."

She sat up straight and stared into those damn deep blue eyes of his, refusing to let herself fall under their spell. "That's just it, Lincoln. I don't know if I can trust anyone. I thought Lawrence loved me, but it was bullshit. My father cares about himself more than my interests. I'm sick of people taking advantage of me."

Lincoln dropped her strand of hair, and a scowl marred his gorgeous face. "Is that what you think? That I've been taking advantage of you?"

Cecily grabbed his hand out of fear he would bolt. "Wait. That's *not* what I think at all." She held tight to his hand. "Last night, I was all set to come in here and tell you I was falling in love with you. I was going to tell you we could give the relationship thing a shot."

"What changed?"

"I'm scared, okay? Everything I believed to be true isn't. I feel like I can't trust anybody right now, not even you. I just need some time—."

Lincoln ripped his hand from hers and stood up. "Time? I think we're out of time, sweetheart. Sorry." He spun on his heel, pushed past the server carrying their food, and walked out of the restaurant.

Chapter 20

Lincoln

His hands shook as he drove. After all this time, after everything he'd done, Cecily still didn't trust him. What more could he do to prove his love to her?

Why did I think this time would be different?

A horn blared behind him, drawing his attention back to the road. He swerved over the double yellow line, one tire in the other lane, before he twisted the wheel and skidded to a stop on the shoulder. He put the truck in park and scrubbed a hand over his face.

This is bullshit.

There was a reason he didn't get involved with a woman for longer than one night. Relationships were nothing more than a punch to the gut. The pain and the heartache were too much. He should have learned his lesson after Cat. Love worked its way into your heart and then blew it to pieces.

"I never should have told her how I felt," he muttered to himself. "So much for honesty."

He ignored the voice in his head telling him to calm down and not jump to conclusions. That voice hadn't helped when he divulged his feelings for Cecily; it wouldn't help him now. He had to face the truth. If Cecily believed he was like Claude and Lawrence, there was nothing else he could do.

Lincoln checked his watch. If he hurried, he could get to the condo, pack, and be on the road within the hour. He wanted Lakeside in his rearview mirror as soon as possible. The sooner he got out of town, the sooner he could get Cecily Devereaux out of his system.

Back on the road, he concentrated on driving through the small town. He hadn't thought it possible, but he was going to miss this place. Small-town life suited him, more than he'd ever imagined. The leisurely pace with which people lived their lives appealed to him. Deep down, he'd thought he could make a life in Lakeside, and part of him hoped that life would include Cecily.

If only…

He stopped himself from going down that rabbit hole. "If only" would tear him apart. No sense dwelling on what could have been; he needed to look forward.

Lincoln eased into the parking spot beside the condo. If he hurried, he could be out of Lakeside before dark and on the road to Missoula. He'd stay in a hotel on Reserve Street and board his plane bright and early tomorrow morning. Before too long, Cecily would be a distant memory.

Inside the condo, he went straight to the bedroom and shoved his clothes in his duffel bag. A quick stop in the bathroom for his toothpaste and deodorant, then he was back to the bedroom for one last look around.

Two sharp raps on the door drew him from the bedroom. He zipped his duffel bag shut, hefted it over his shoulder, and pulled open the door.

"Hi," Serena said. "You got a minute?"

"Sure," Lincoln nodded. "Come on in."

Serena shook her head and pointed over her shoulder. "Can we talk out here?"

He stepped outside and pulled the door closed behind him. He forgot Serena hadn't stepped foot in her condo since her abusive ex-boyfriend had attacked her inside and tried to kidnap her. Asshole move on his part.

"Sorry."

She smiled at him. "It's okay." Serena cleared her throat. "Van and I are heading out on the boat. We thought you might want to come with us."

Lincoln shook his head. "I don't think so. I'm leaving." He dug the condo keys out of his pocket and handed them to her.

Serena scowled as she stared at the keys in her hand. "I thought you were staying for a couple more days."

"I'm catching a flight out of Missoula early tomorrow morning. I'm leaving Lakeside tonight to stay in Missoula." He shrugged. "It's the easiest thing to do."

"I don't understand," she said. "What about Cecily?"

"Cecily has a lot going on right now. She found out some stuff about her father and his involvement in her engagement."

"Hey!" Van jogged across the street, Soldier on his heels. "What's going on?" He glanced at the duffel bag in Lincoln's hand. "Are you leaving?"

"Yeah."

"Did you talk to Cecily? Tell her what we discovered about Lawrence?"

Lincoln nodded. "She already knew, though."

"She did?" Van said. "How? I had to dig deep to find out he was Fortuna's son."

Lincoln explained his conversation with Cecily and what she had discovered. Once he was done, he said, "So, as you can see, it's probably best for both of us if I give her some space and time to figure out what she wants."

Van crossed his arms over his chest and shook his head. "Whenever you say you want to give a woman time to figure out what she wants, that's Lincoln speak for 'I'm done with this before it gets serious.'"

"Van—."

His friend held up his hand. "You know how I always bitch about it bugging me that you know me so well? Well, guess what? *I* know *you*, Linc, and you're bailing. When it gets hard, you bolt."

Lincoln shot Van a dirty look, tossed his bag in the truck, and slammed the door. "Cecily made it clear she isn't interested in a relationship."

Serena stomped her foot and glared at him. "She said she needed time; that's not the same as not being interested in a relationship. Give her a chance."

Lincoln glanced at Van, but his friend stared past him at the lake, his hand resting on Soldier's head.

"You're right, Serena. But I don't think she wants a relationship, especially after everything she just discovered. Besides, it's been two weeks. I think that's enough time. If she doesn't know what she wants by now, she never will."

"That's not fair," Serena snapped. "She just got devastating news. You can't ask her to make a life-altering decision right now."

"Can you help me here?" Lincoln pleaded with his best friend.

Van shook his head. "Nope. She's got a point. Cecily's father is an ass, her ex-fiancé is an ass, and she literally just discovered they were co-conspirators to control her life. She deserves some time to figure out what she wants."

So much for friendship. Lincoln looked at his watch and yanked open the truck door. "I gotta go. I want to get to Missoula before dark."

"Why don't you stay two or three more days, maybe talk to Cecily again?" Van suggested. "We don't mind. You can stay in Serena's condo for as long as you want."

"I need to get home," Lincoln muttered.

Serena gave him a dirty look, spun on her heel, and stomped across the street. He didn't enjoy making her angry—it wasn't his intention—but he needed to get out of Montana and get his head on straight. He turned to Van.

"Your wife is mad at me."

"She'll be fine. I'll talk to her."

"Will you explain to her—?"

"I'll try. I can't promise she won't still be mad at you, though. Go home to New York and figure out what *you* want. I know that's what you want and need to do." Van held out his hand.

Lincoln grabbed it and pulled him into a hug. "Thank you." He took a deep breath. "I'll be back, I swear."

"I know."

Lincoln crouched down, took Soldier's head in his hands, and scratched the dog behind his ears. He gave him one last pat, stood up, and climbed into the truck. As he turned the corner, he looked in the rearview mirror and saw Van raise his hand in a half-hearted wave.

Chapter 21

Cecily

Cecily stared at the picture of her father and mother on their wedding day. It was one of the few times she'd seen her father with a sincere smile on his face.

What happened to him?

Her mother wouldn't know the man her father had become. A tear slid down her cheek, and she brushed it away. She missed her mother every day, but lately it had been an indescribable ache. Her father never understood her, but her mother always had her back. When Claude Devereaux was being his worst and making Cecily's life impossible, Deirdre Devereaux made things better.

"Cecily."

Her father stood in the doorway with Lawrence right behind him, peering over his shoulder with a salacious, triumphant smirk on his face.

She pushed herself to her feet and stepped around the desk. "Daddy. I see you brought Lawrence along."

Her father strode into the room, his head held high, his shoulders back, and a fierce scowl on his face. "Don't start, young lady."

Cecily sighed. "I came back to New York to discuss the letter you left me."

"I assume that means you've come to your senses. Your old position is still available with the company. I secured a temporary lease on an apartment overlooking Central Park for you, and I arranged a tour of the Four Seasons next week as a potential wedding venue."

She crossed her arms and dug her nails into her biceps, a reminder not to let her father intimidate her. It irked her that he assumed she was prepared to do as he said. She glanced at Lawrence, now smirking in the corner, and cleared her throat.

"I'm here to discuss Gerald Fortuna."

Lawrence coughed and, for a brief second, her father's tightly controlled façade slipped. Claude clenched his fists, and his shoulders sagged the tiniest bit. He pulled himself together before he spoke.

"I do not know what you are talking about."

Cecily opened her briefcase, pulled out the folder of information she carried all the way from Lakeside, and dropped it in the center of Claude's desk. Her heart pounded, and her palms were sweating.

Her father didn't move. He stared at the folder on the desk, his lower lip caught between his teeth. When he looked up, it wasn't Cecily he looked at but Lawrence.

"Lawrence, please excuse us?"

"I—."

"Now, Lawrence."

He huffed, but he did as Claude asked. He paused at the door, glanced back at Cecily with a pinched look on his face, then he opened the door, stepped out, and slammed it.

She turned around to find her father sitting at his desk with the folder open, flipping through the papers. She eased into the chair across from him and waited.

It took Claude almost ten minutes to go through the folder. When he was done, he closed it and sat back in his chair.

"Where did you find this?"

Cecily shrugged. "I looked for it, Daddy. After reading your letter, including the line about an 'alliance' with Lawrence, it occurred to me why you pushed this engagement so hard. I'm not as stupid as you think."

"Obviously." He shifted in his seat. Cecily had never seen her father so uncomfortable. "I wish I could say this isn't what it looks like, but clearly it's not worth denying."

"You're right. There is no need to deny it."

Claude folded his hands on top of the desk and squeezed his eyes closed. "What do you want?"

"I want to be left alone. I don't want you interfering in my life anymore."

Her father opened his eyes. "That's it?"

Cecily nodded. "What else could I possibly want from you?"

Claude sighed. "A job? Money? That stupid island in the middle of nowhere? You don't want anything?"

"I don't want to be beholden to you for anything," she snapped. "It would be more stuff for you to hold over my head and another way to make me miserable."

"How did we get to this point?" he whispered. "You're my little girl. I love you."

Tears pricked the corner of her eyes. "You haven't said that in a long time."

Claude sighed, and his shoulders slumped. He leaned back in his chair. "After your mother died, I wasn't sure I could love anymore. She was my entire world. My everything." Claude scrubbed a hand over his face. "The biggest mistake I ever made was shutting you out. My focus was on the business. I lost touch with you and thought supporting the engagement to Lawrence would bring us closer. It didn't matter how or why the engagement happened, only that it did. I thought you were happy. Or maybe I so desperately wanted you to be happy that I was blind to the fact that you weren't."

"Even though I told you time and time again I wasn't happy with Lawrence, you wouldn't let it go. You kept pushing me to stay with him and to marry him. Keeping your business solvent was more important than my happiness."

Claude shook his head. "It wasn't, I swear."

Cecily sighed. "You know what's funny about all of this? If you had come to me and told me what was going on, I might have been able to help you. We could have figured something out." She waved her finger in a circle. "We could have saved all of this, saved Devereaux Industries. Together." She rose to her feet, walked around the desk, and kissed her father on the cheek. "I'm going back to my life in Montana."

She turned to leave, but her father grabbed her hand and stopped her. "Wait."

"There's nothing else to say."

"Maybe there is. Maybe there is still a way to save my company. *Our* company." He hit the intercom button on the phone. "Becca, could you get a lawyer from the legal department in here, please? As quick as possible."

"What are you doing?" Cecily asked.

"Righting my wrongs," Claude replied.

———

Cecily's face hurt from smiling. She had expected to walk into Devereaux Industries, tell her father off, and walk out destitute and homeless. Instead, she carried paperwork in her briefcase that gave her a controlling interest in her father's company. Now it was her company.

To say it shocked her would be an understatement. Not only had Claude signed over his interest in the company to her, but he also agreed to step down for the good of the company. Her head spun with all the things she needed to do. She would have to stay in New York for at least a month to get everything squared away.

"Cecily!"

Lawrence slid to a stop in front of her. She had hoped to make it out of the building without running into him, but luck was not on her side.

"What did you do?"

She feigned ignorance. "I'm sorry? I'm not sure what you're talking about."

"Your father told me to clean out my desk and be out of the building by the end of the day. What the hell is going on? Two hours ago, he told me you and I were getting married, and he would put me on the board. Now I'm fired?"

"To be fair, it wasn't my father who fired you; it was me. He delivered the message, but I made the final decision."

Lawrence took a step back. "You can't do that."

Cecily's smile widened. "Oh, but I can. I now hold the controlling interest in Devereaux Industries." She wiggled her briefcase. "The lawyer is filing the paperwork as we speak. First on my agenda is removing any trace of you and your mob boss father from my company."

Lawrence grunted and took a step toward her. "Do it, and you'll regret it. Trust me."

Cecily didn't back down; instead, she stepped closer until she was mere inches from Lawrence's face. "I'm not afraid of your father, Lawrence. Not even a little. His hold over Devereaux Industries is finished."

Lawrence blinked and backed up. He spun on his heel and walked away without a word. Cecily watched him until he got on the elevator, then she crossed the lobby to the security desk and got the attention of the young lady sitting at the monitors.

"Yes, Ms. Devereaux?"

"Can you make sure Lawrence Bronson is out of the building by five p.m., please?"

The woman nodded. "Of course, Ms. Devereaux."

"Please, call me Cecily." She pulled off her visitor's badge, set it on the counter, and walked out the door.

———

For the third night in a row, she walked to the bar down the street from her hotel. She sat in the same spot, ordered the same drink, and kept her eyes on the door. She deflected the attention of other patrons, politely declining offers to buy her a drink or take her on the dance floor. After two hours, she dropped some money on the bar and left.

Call him.

The little voice in her head wouldn't shut up, no matter how often she told it to be quiet. The problem was the voice was right. She should call him. Hoping to run into Lincoln at the bar where they met was a lesson in futility. If she just picked up the phone and told him she was in town and wanted to see him, he would come.

Maybe.

"Shut up," she muttered under her breath.

It had been six weeks since she'd seen Lincoln or spoken to him. Cecily *wanted* to call him. She wanted to talk to him, kiss him, make love to him, *be* with him. But the thought scared her. Hell, it terrified her.

What was she supposed to say? "I'm sorry" wasn't enough, and "I'm ready now" seemed lame. She'd asked for time, and he'd given it to her. Eight weeks. There had been no communication—no texts, emails, or phone calls. Not that she hadn't picked her phone up dozens of times, intent on calling him or at least texting him, but one day bled into another and another until her one-month stay in New York had turned into two.

She stepped into the elevator, hit the number five on the panel, and stabbed repeatedly at the button to close the door until it eased shut. She pulled her phone out of her purse and checked for messages: five from her administrative assistant, one from her father, and another from her lawyer, but nothing from Lincoln. Cecily unlocked her room, tossed the phone on the bed, and grabbed her suitcase from the closet. Her plane left at eight tomorrow morning, so she wanted to get packed tonight.

Tomorrow she would be home, back in Montana. There was still a lot of work to do, but she'd put a great New York team in place, and she knew she could do the same in Lakeside. She couldn't wait to get home. She missed her dog, the Tuttles, and the island.

Cecily sat on the bed with her phone in her hand and stared at the screen. It was now or never. She hit the button, put the phone to her ear, and waited.

"You've reached Lincoln Dunn. Please leave a message, and I'll get back to you as soon as possible."

She cleared her throat. "Um, hi, Lincoln. It's me. Cecily. I, uh, wanted to say hi." She closed her eyes and took a deep breath. "I miss you. I'd love it if you called me back."

Cecily ended the call, packed her bags, and showered, then she crawled into bed and pulled the blankets up to her chin. Lincoln was front and center in her mind as she drifted off to sleep.

Chapter 22

Lincoln

Lincoln stopped dead in his tracks, unable to look away from the beauty in front of him. He crouched down and held out his hand. The tiny ball of fur stretched out its neck and sniffed his fingers.

"She's cute, isn't she?" the young lady sitting on the park bench said.

Lincoln smiled. "She's adorable. Is she a Shih Tzu?"

The girl nodded. "Her name is Sadie." She licked her lips. "I don't suppose you're interested in a dog, are you? I'm trying to find her a home."

"You're getting rid of her?"

"She's the last of the litter. Unbelievably sweet, even-tempered, and housebroken. Obviously, she likes you."

Lincoln laughed. "You're a great salesperson."

The girl shrugged. "I don't have to be when she's so cute." She narrowed her eyes. "Are you interested?"

An hour later, he walked out of the PetSmart on Broadway with three bags of dog necessities—a bed, toys, food, harness, leash, dog bath products, a crate, and training treats. He juggled them and his new dog as he hailed a cab. He kept Sadie tucked under his arm while she surveyed the world around her. Now and then, she would lick his arm, either to remind him she was there or to make sure he was real; he wasn't sure which.

The doorman at his building—Arnold—raised a wary eyebrow when he climbed from the cab, but he hurried over to help him pull everything out of the cab.

"Mr. Dunn, what did you do?"

"I bought myself a dog." Lincoln held her up, as if Arnold hadn't already noticed her. "She's cute, huh? Her name is Sadie."

Arnold shook his head. "I hope you know what you're in for. Puppies are like newborn babies. I don't think you'll be getting much sleep."

Lincoln didn't have the heart to tell him he hadn't been sleeping much anyway, not since leaving Lakeside. Maybe Sadie would bring him some peace. He kissed the top of her head.

"She'll be a good girl, won't you, Miss Sadie?"

"You're smitten," Arnold laughed. "It's nice to see you smile, sir."

"Thanks, Arnold. It's, uh, nice to smile again." He cleared his throat. "Can you get all this stuff upstairs for me? I'm going to take her for a walk."

He took the harness and leash out of the bag and put them on Sadie. He set her on the ground and burst out laughing when she twisted herself up in the leash and flopped down on the ground.

"Don't worry, baby girl; we'll work on it."

Lincoln coaxed her down the street. It took Sadie a few minutes, but she got the hang of it about five blocks from his apartment. They were a hundred yards from the bar where he met Cecily—a place he'd avoided for two months—when he noticed a curvy, raven-haired woman come out the door.

Holy shit. Cecily.

Before he could even think about yelling Cecily's name, Sadie turned around and darted between his legs, tangling her leash around his ankles. Lincoln grunted and slid to a stop, one hand on the wall beside to keep himself from falling to the ground. He swore under his breath, snatched up the puppy, and untangled himself. When he looked up, the woman was nowhere to be seen.

"Probably just my imagination," he muttered.

Lincoln tucked Sadie under his arm and headed back to his apartment. Arnold had taken everything upstairs and left it on his kitchen table. Beside it was the day's paper, folded neatly in half. He put Sadie on the floor so she could explore, grabbed a beer from the fridge, and set to work putting away her things.

He couldn't stop thinking about Cecily. While he didn't think the black-haired woman that he saw leaving the bar was her, it had certainly dredged up memories. Not a day went by that he didn't think about Cecily. As much as he hated to admit it, he missed her. Coming home to New York was supposed to get her out of his system and he was supposed to move on, but he found himself stuck, unable to do anything other than regret the choices he made.

Maybe I should call her.

Lincoln chastised himself for even considering it. Cecily hadn't contacted him, which solidified his belief that she was not interested in a relationship with him. Calling her would only end in heartache. He was sure of it.

He grabbed the paper and moved to the couch. A few seconds after he sat down, the tiny Shih Tzu wandered over, curled up on his feet, and fell asleep. He chuckled and scratched the top of her head. Van would lose his mind when he found out Lincoln had bought a dog. He couldn't wait to tell him.

He searched for his phone so he could call his best friend, but the headline under the fold of the newspaper caught his eye.

Devereaux Industries Taken Over by Billionaire Entrepreneur's Daughter.

He snatched up the paper and skimmed the article. According to the story, Claude Devereaux had signed over control of his company to Cecily two months earlier. She swooped in and made broad changes across the company, which included ending a long-term financial arrangement with Fortuna Financial, a company owned by the known mobster, Gerald Fortuna.

"I'm bringing integrity back to Devereaux Industries," they quoted Cecily. "This will be a company people will be proud to work for, one that will make money, and one that will lead the business world into the future. I can't wait to get started."

They filled the article with glowing comments about Cecily and her plans for the company, which included moving the CEO offices out of cold, impersonal New York and to her adopted hometown in Montana. She was confident it would go well because she had put a crack team in place to keep the New York office running. Technology would allow her to be part of the business from the other side of the country.

"Wow, nice work, sweetheart," he whispered. "I knew you could stand up to your father."

The puppy's head popped up, and she stared at Lincoln with her big brown eyes. He picked her up and set her in his lap. She curled up and went back to sleep.

Lincoln rubbed his hand down her back, ruffling her soft fur. "You know what, Sadie? I have a friend named Sebastian who I think you would like."

His cellphone beeped from the kitchen table, but Sadie looked so comfortable, he opted not to get up. He would check it later.

"Are you ready for this?" Van asked.

Lincoln laughed. "Is anybody ever ready for something like this?"

Van laughed along with him. "True. You got everything you need?"

Lincoln patted the bag sitting on the floor by his feet. "I think so."

"Call me if you need me to bail you out."

"Of jail?"

Van snorted. "Well, if things don't go as planned, you might *need* bail money."

"Ha-ha." Lincoln opened the truck door and climbed out. He grabbed the bag from the floor, double-checked to make sure he had everything he needed, and headed inside.

He'd put a lot of thought into how the next few minutes of his life would play out. The decision hadn't been an easy one, but it was the right one. He just wished it hadn't taken him three months to figure out what he needed to do.

It took a minute for his eyes to adjust after he stepped inside. He only took a few steps inside the Time Out Bar and Grill before he sat at a table by the door. He hefted his bag onto the table with a grunt and unzipped it.

Sadie popped her head out. She'd grown a lot in the last month, putting on three pounds since he'd brought her home. She licked his face and gave him her adorable grin.

"Hey, Sadie Sue. You're a good girl, aren't you?" He straightened the bow on her collar, attached her leash to her harness, and took her out of her carrier. He took the folded papers out of the side of the bag, tucked them into his back pocket, checked his front pocket one more time, and then set Sadie on the floor.

"Come on, girl."

Sebastian noticed him first. He bounded to his feet, rushed across the bar, jumped up, and put his paws on Lincoln's leg. He barked once.

"Hey, buddy! It's good to see you." He reached down and petted the little white dog. "No more cast, huh?"

"He got it off last month," Cecily said.

Her voice was music to his ears. He closed his eyes for a second before he opened them and smiled at her.

"Hey, Lincoln."

"Hey, gorgeous. How's it going?"

Cecily grinned. "Good. Great." She hopped off her barstool, kneeled, and held out her hand. "Who is this little one?"

"That is Sadie. I thought her and Sebastian could be friends."

Sebastian ducked under Cecily's hand and sniffed Sadie's ear. He stretched, rested his head on his paws, and barked. Cecily patted his flank, whispered "be nice," and stood up.

"Oh, yeah?" She tipped her head to one side. "Are you planning on hanging around long enough for them to become friends?"

Lincoln pointed at the barstools. "Can we talk for a minute?"

Cecily nodded and eased onto the stool she'd just vacated. Lincoln sat beside her and cleared his throat.

"Congratulations on acquiring your father's company," he said.

"Thanks." Her smile widened. "I thought it was time for me to stand up to my father and let him know who was in charge of my life."

Lincoln laughed. "Just like you said you would. Is everything going well?"

"It's getting there. We have a lot of work to get done, a lot of changes to make, but it's coming together. I'm excited about the future."

"You should be."

"Thank you." She took a sip of her drink. "Now, what did you want to discuss?"

He pulled the papers from his back pocket, unfolded them, and slid them across the bar to Cecily.

"What is this?"

"Read it."

She picked up the papers, her eyes widening as she read them. When she was done, she swallowed, gripped the papers tightly in both hands, and turned to look at him.

"Lincoln?"

He put his hand over hers. "It's a prenuptial agreement."

"I know what it is. What I want to know is why? What are you ... what are you doing?"

"I want you to trust me. This was the only way I know how to prove to you I *can* be trusted." He tapped the paper in her hand. "I'm not interested in your money or your company. My only interest is you."

Cecily bit her lower lip. "This might be the most romantic thing anybody's ever done for me." She turned her hand over and took hold of his.

"One more thing." With his free hand, Lincoln reached into his front pocket and pulled out the velvet box. He opened it and set it in front of Cecily. "It's not an engagement, not yet anyway, but it is a promise." He leaned close, his lips brushing her the shell of her ear. "I love you, Cecily Devereaux. And I promise to love you for as long as you want me. Forever, if that's what you want."

"Forever sounds good," Cecily whispered. "In fact, it sounds a lot better than a two-week one-night stand."

Lincoln laughed, took hold of her chin, and pulled her close. His mouth closed over hers, and it was the best kiss they ever shared; it was the kiss that sealed the promise.

THE END

Follow Mimi Francis at mimifrancis.com to stay in the loop. Subscribe to her newsletter for exclusive news and stories.

Book Club Questions:

1. If you had to trade places with one character in this book, who would it be? Why?

2. How did the setting impact the story? Would you want to read more books set in Lakeside, Montana? Would you want to visit Lakeside based on this book?

3. If you were making a movie of this book, who would you cast as Lincoln? How about as Cecily?

4. If you had to pick another character to be the protagonist, who would it be? Why?

5. To which character did you most relate or empathize?

6. Did Lawrence make a good "villain"?

7. Which dog was your favorite? Soldier, Sebastian, or Sadie? Which one would you want as a pet?

8. If you were Cecily, what would you do when you found out what her father did?

9. Were you rooting for Lincoln and Cecily to get together? Why or why not?

10. What songs did you think of while reading this book? (For extra fun: make a playlist!)

Author Bio

Mimi Francis writes contemporary romance of the spicy, steamy variety. She loves writing tropes and frequently uses them in her series, *Second Chances in Hollywood* and *Loves of Lakeside*. Mimi stumbled into writing when her favorite obsessions—Marvel and *Supernatural*—led her to writing fan fiction. With encouragement from friends, family, and her fan fiction readers, she successfully made the jump to writing original fiction.

When she's not writing, she works as an administrative assistant, crochets, binge-watches her favorite TV shows and movies, and spends time with her three children, Ariana, Tiana, and Giovanni, her four dogs, and her husband of twenty-eight years, Frank.

More books from 4 Horsemen Publications

Romance

Ann Shepphird
The War Council

Emily Bunney
All or Nothing
All the Way
All Night Long: Novella
All She Needs
Having it All
All at Once
All Together
All for Her

KT Bond
Back to Life
Back to Love
Back at Last

Lynn Chantale
The Baker's Touch
Blind Secrets
Broken Lens
Blind Fury
Time Bomb

VIP's Revenge
Chef's Taste

Mandy Fate
Love Me, Goaltender
Captain of My Heart

Mimi Francis
Private Lives
Private Protection
Private Party
Run Away Home
The Professor
Our Two-Week, One-Night Stand

Shae Coon
Bound in Love
Controlling Assets
For His Own Protection
Her Broken Pieces
The Roma's Claim
The Roma's Promise